FEAR NOT THE JACKAL

FEAR NOT THE JACKAL

Miles DeMott

This book is a work of fiction. Any references to historical events, real people, or real locations are made in the spirit of fictional creation. All other names, characters, places, and incidents are the sole fabrication of the author's imagination, and any resemblance to real or actual people or places or events is coincidental.

No part of this book may be reproduced in any form or by any electronic or mechanical means including information storage and retrieval systems, without permission in writing from the author. The only exception is by a reviewer, who may quote short excerpts in a review.

Copyright 2012 © Miles DeMott.
All rights reserved.
www.milesdemott.com

Printed in the United States of America.

Book design and layout by 24 Communications. www.24c.co
Cover image by Elmore DeMott. www.elmoredemott.com

ISBN 978-0-9829358-4-2 (paperback)
ISBN 978-0-9829358-5-9 (eBook)

Give this book as a gift!

Available in trade paper and electronic versions for iBooks, Nook and Kindle.

To give this book as a gift, visit the bookstore at www.milesdemott.com.

For my sisters

June 27, 1974

The whir of the helicopter blades was intoxicating, and I couldn't take my eyes off of the complex instrument panel that held the pilot's attention as much as my own. Once I had gotten over the fear of lifting off and watching the ground retreat beneath us, I had begun to entertain the notion that one day I would fly. Maybe not helicopters, but something. I watched the instruments so intently that I hardly noticed the scenery we had chosen the helicopter ride to see, as beneath us the Grand Canyon spread in all directions. I'm sure it was pretty, but this was 1974, and my family was in the middle of its annual summer vacation, the one week during the year that my father was willing to leave the pharmacy in search of family connection.

We stretched across most of the wide seat, window to window on the front of the two vinyl-covered benches reserved for tourists. Behind us were two couples from Michigan. I remember that they talked funny. My family occupied all but one of the seats on our bench, the window seat by the cargo door occupied by a quiet man who had been the last to board. Next to him, in order, sat my older sister Janine, then me, my mother Faye, father Archie, and younger brother Thibodeaux. My parents had tried to sit toward the middle to allow better views for their children, though their plan had been partially foiled by the late arrival of the quiet man by the window. For me, though, the view was straight ahead, between the pilot and the tour guide who kept turning back and forth between the passengers and the instruments, his mouth hidden by a giant foam microphone attached to a headset just like the ones we were wearing to hear about the power of water against sandstone.

The helicopter had risen to mysterious star status on the evening news, ever-present in the war footage shipped home from a place I couldn't find on a map. Those copters had guns and soldiers hanging out of the doors like G.I. JOE, the pilots wearing helmets and appearing cool and collected under enemy fire. On that June day, I was the pilot, steering the helicopter through the jungle-less landscape of the canyons as the Colorado River rushed below. I leaned with the pilot's control stick and mirrored his eyes as they scanned the instruments and the horizon. I was not interested in the view to the sides, and Janine didn't seem to be either, having been forced to leave her boyfriend behind at home and suffer social separation along with family connection. She had pouted for most of the trip, so it never occurred to me that she might've wanted the seat next to the window. I wanted the middle seat, claimed the middle seat, and remained so intently focused on the instrument panel that I didn't notice her unbuckle her seat belt and only felt the brush of her leg as she rose slightly to exchange seats with the quiet man who had offered her the seat. She had, I would learn later, even looked behind my back to my mother to gain approval for the swap.

All of that happened behind me as I leaned with the pilot to climb out over the canyon wall, and I was aware of nothing until I felt the rush of wind to my right and turned in time to watch as the quiet man held the door handle with his right hand and Janine by the waist of her bell-bottom jeans with his left hand

and launched them both through the wide open cargo door, her grip on the doorframe no match for the downward prop wash or the quiet man's death wish, and her eyes wide with mortal terror. I passed a confused look from the cargo door back to my mother, having only caught the last second of the strange sequence of events, but she only screamed in silent anguish, fumbling with her own seatbelt and trying to climb over me as the tour guide made every effort to secure the door. It didn't occur to me until much later that day, after they had recovered her body downriver, that Janine wasn't coming back, that Thib and I were now two where there had been three, and that the hole in our family created by her fall would get a lot bigger before it got any better.

August 11, 2009

"Damn," was the initial response but probably not the only thought mustered by the naked female form on the bed next to me, inhaling a cigarette and the old family narrative as a sliver of light crept through the pulled plastic shades and danced across the stippled ceiling of Room 345 of any of a million business hotels along my mid-life journey. I was at once reminded of my fondness for my wife's curiosity, and the fact that she didn't smoke. "That's a bummer." Twenty-somethings often captured the essence of a moment so economically.

As I swung my legs over the side of the bed searching for stability, the clock radio's indication of 1:43 AM was the sole light on the bedside table, though I glanced at the phone's dark message light out of habit and ran my hands through my hair, resting my elbows on my knees before using the combination to lever myself upright in the direction of the bathroom. The fluorescent tubes sputtered to life with the soft click of a switch, casting a blueish hew on graying temples framing bloodshot eyes looking through me to the shower curtain behind and the hopeless and fleeting thought of washing this latest transgression from the record. Instead, I grabbed Judas by the neck and drained about three hours of whiskey into the guilty stream no doubt flowing from the rest of the building, flushing another bad decision out of my system, closing my eyes and shaking my head slowly while recounting the evening's events: driving through the rainy summer night, exiting the interstate at the typical oasis of chain hotels and restaurants that cater to the road warriors of large commerce, making the usual small talk with the young gal at the reception desk, and again with increased intensity after a late and predominantly liquid supper at the neighborhood grill next door, leading to the midnight knock and the gymnastics that followed.

Would that this were a new story, a recent development that might lend some spice to the encounter, escort it to something that could transcend the purely biological, analogous to the rite of older pine trees producing more pine cones to cast more seeds into the face of their inevitable demise. But that would be too easy. I had become that guy. I was the cliche. And while I was not the only person, man or woman, to reach this evolutionary waypoint, I was the only one standing in that bathroom prosecuting the little head for the crimes of the big.

I returned to an empty bed and tried to be attentive as Brittany or Amber or Melissa undressed in reverse, far less seductively than she had a couple of hours before, while presenting a litany of reasons for her sense of urgency where none was needed. When she returned to the edge of the bed to put on her shoes, she paused long enough to look over her now fully clothed shoulder and ask a question.

"Did that really happen to your sister?" she asked, her eyes dashing in and out of the sliver of curtain light, a moving target for an old gun.

"What, you think I made that up?" I replied with thinly veiled sarcasm.

"I don't know," she said, returning to her laces and raising the other foot to repeat the process. "I don't know you at all. I mean, we lay down some pretty good tracks and then you spring this heavy shit, like, out of the blue. What am I supposed to make of that?"

"Not a damn thing, I suppose," was my weak response. "I can't even say why it came to mind. I can say it's true, though."

"It's like I'm supposed to be your sister because I'm younger than you? And this is some metaphor for some kind of fucked up helicopter thing you got going? Cause that's really creepy."

"It's nothing like that, let me assure you," I replied quickly, beginning to wonder where she was going with this line of questioning, rising up on one elbow to decrease the distance between us and re-establish a connection that seemed to be waning all too rapidly, sliding quickly from passion to litigation. "It really did happen, but it was a long time ago," I finished, immediately regretting the reference to the age difference.

She turned to face me again, lacing complete, and the sliver of parking lot light split her face between the eyes, the brightness bleeding over just enough to hide the edges and the ears. She seemed to reconcile the events in that light and leaned over to punctuate our time together with a hesitant kiss, as if required to do so because the people in the movies always seemed to do that.

"I had a good time," she said. "You're pretty charming for an old guy." And with the final word she was gone, checking her cell phone as she disappeared through the door and down the hall, leaving me to regain my breath and collapse into low-thread-count linens and the realization that some itches just can't be scratched.

Moments later, relatively speaking, the clock radio on the small table between the beds began screeching its cacophonous digital alarm. Without really waking, I was able to find the industry standard snooze button that allocated an additional seven minutes to what had been the fitful sleep of the middle aged, tossing punctuated by turning, a dance to the music of highway sounds, white noise, and the quiet refrain of frequent urination. Rubbing what felt like mortar from the corners of my eyes, I ran the palms of my hands across the cheeky stubble and combed my hair back with my fingers, clasped my hands behind my head and allowed my eyes to adjust to the morning light, counting the snoozed minutes that had stayed the execution of the day's beginning.

The stippled ceiling, in the daylight, now took on new meaning, appeared almost to mimic the spine of the Appalachians in topographical relief, before the interstate system created cloverleafs and intersections where enterprising real estate developers carved out pads for shiny new old-fashioned country stores that courted passing tourists and wooed locals from former town centers now struggling to redirect growth toward the vital arteries. I followed the spine of a particularly generous dollop of squished sheetrock mud into a circular valley not unlike the one surrounded by the foothills of North Georgia where my grandfather had ministered to the hardscrabble country folks that preceded the outlet malls and gated communities of the new religious. His gift with a split bamboo fly rod was legendary among the early visitors to the trout streams that ran unimpeded through those valleys, and I could almost paint small blue lines along the ceiling and picture the old man walking along the banks, pants and sleeves rolled up, bright eyes searching pools and eddies for fishy movement.

The pleasant memories were interrupted by an exposed seam in the prefabricated ceiling, a straight and logical intrusion on the circuitous and thoughtfully reflective moment, and the hills and valleys of my grandfather's North Georgia were ushered out by the bulldozers of suburban creep. After all, those who dedicated resources in the path of progress typically won, and some of them won big, and lost big, only to win big again. Vicious cycle ridden by vicious men. Business is business.

But today's business was not to be decided on the battlefield of commercial linens, so I hoisted my frame up once again, silenced the pending alarm—a small victory to start the day—and padded across the low-pile carpet into the fluorescent cave once again to take up arms against my reflection, to grapple with my humanity, and most importantly, to shit, shower, and shave.

I'd like to say that it wasn't until breakfast, a combination of waffle and scrambled cheese eggs at one of the exit's two Waffle Houses, that the gravity of the evening's transgressions really hit me, and I'd like to attribute that realization to the fact that my wife called to let me know that the plumber could not find the leak in the steam generator and was asking what I wanted to do about it. But such an admission was about as likely as my wife repairing the steam shower herself. We would both, instead, revert back to role dyads that society, it would seem, had wired us for. She prattled on about the plumber and a thousand other flaws in our master bathroom, all of which needed immediate attention, while I listened with interest, offered affirmative, monosyllabic utterances of agreement, and watched the second hand of my watch auger slowly into my wrist, willing the waffle iron to quicken its pace so the day could officially begin and unapologetically require my full attention. So many words. So little sex.

"You want syrup or honey with that waffle, Hon?" The waitress's whispered voice drew my attention away from the phone long enough to indicate syrup, then returned to close the call.

"Honey, I have to go. My breakfast is here. Tell Irving I'll get back to him about the steam shower, but I need to do some research first." The waitress returned with the syrup. "I hear what you're saying, but there's nothing I can do about it from here. I'll get to it as quickly as I can." I shouldered the phone and spread the butter across the top of the waffle. "Love you, too."

Before you go calling me a cold, heartless bastard—if there's still time—it might help you to understand that facades were actually my specialty. Early in my adult life it became evident that certain lines of work meshed perfectly with my unique psychological profile. It would be romantic to suggest that this match resulted in a successful career as an assassin or a neurosurgeon or a kindergarten teacher, all of which also require very discrete personality types. It was different for me, though. For some reason, it always seemed to be different for me, and I had spent the bulk of my adult life, up to that point at least, in the real estate business developing one strip mall after another, lifestyle center after lifestyle center, lease upon lease, anchor to anchor. I measured my progress not in time or revenue but in square feet. I recognize that my occupation does not excuse my abysmal behavior, but the pursuit of excuses has never really excited me much. Time has taught me that blame for domestic dysfunction is rarely unilateral, and that time is often a lousy teacher.

The connection was immediate for me. The minute the plane took off from the small executive airport outside of Charlotte, I knew why the memory of my sister's death had come scratching its way back from where I diligently compartmentalized it to the top of my consciousness. I had never really been comfortable with small planes and helicopters after that trip to the Grand Canyon, even though such plane rides had become fairly commonplace in my professional life. This morning's flight around the west side of Charlotte had been planned for more than a week, though I'd never really learned the purpose of it. I assumed, since I was one of the younger heads of only slightly graying hair on the flight, that I was playing a supporting role on whatever the project was to be and therefore didn't need advance information. After all, a mall is a mall is a mall. The opportunity is largely driven by the numbers, and nobody schedules a plane until the numbers work. The details would all be explained in due time, I assumed. And so it was.

"The proposed site encompasses about a thousand acres," Jason Sharp said as he pointed out the window, "though the first couple of phases only use about half of that, including anticipated parking."

The others on the plane continued to look out of the window to the trees below as the pilot did as requested, circling the site in a lazy figure eight to allow all seats a view. I began to do the math in my head, filling in the carrying costs for phases three and four, maybe five? It prompted my first question.

"How many phases, total, and what's the timeline for complete buildout?"

"Looks like a total of four to absorb the entire site," Jason replied almost in passing, still looking out the window, "but the timeline will really depend on the market response."

As I looked down among the trees for the usual confluence of necessaries, I saw the interstates and smaller county roads that skirted the site, but there were very few rooftops, no clear access from the interstate, and no existing retail at all. That prompted the second question.

"Market response is likely to be slow, since it looks like your folks are stepping out on the limb first," I said, pointing out the window as if drawing on a white board. "I don't see any retail whatsoever, and the demographics don't seem to match what the numbers were telling you, because all I see are a lot of trees and small rooftops. This is really pushing the idea of destination retail, in my opinion. Who have you lined up to anchor?"

I turned from the window to look at the others, all of whom were looking at me with furrowed brows, like I had something written on my forehead that they couldn't quite make out. Then the man seated next to Jason, whose name I couldn't immediately recall but remember clearly now as Dan Richards, answered with a smile growing across his face.

"The Lord is our Anchor."

"And how's His credit?" I replied without thinking, recovering quickly to my feet and filling in the gaps in my information on the fly. "Pretty good,

I hear." That last part drew a chuckle that perhaps salvaged my supporting role. Still confused, though, I couldn't figure why I would even play a supporting role if all they were building was a church. That confusion prompted the third and final question.

"Isn't a thousand acres a whole lot for a church to carry?"

The other passengers now looked at each other as if I was indeed the last to know, which, it turns out, I was. The knowing smile crept across the face of Dan Richards once again, and I assumed it did so condescendingly, though as my relationship with him progressed, I came to understand the impossibility of that assumption.

"We're not building a church, Mr. Felder. We're building an experience."

I looked at the other passengers, all of whom looked back at me with expressions of knowledge mixed with excited disbelief, like they were excited about something that they couldn't quite quantify.

"You mean, like an amusement park?" I asked.

"Something like that," Richards replied with hesitation, not wanting that term to enter the discussion but lacking a more analogous option.

"Would that be for His amusement or for yours?" I responded too quickly, the idea of an amusement park for God having never entered into the realm of my imagination. Luckily, the quick response drew a chuckle as well, though it became evident that his fears had been realized.

"Perhaps for both," Richards replied, "though we envision a larger mission than simply amusement."

"Okay," I replied with a deferent nod to him and a cursory glance to the others. "That makes sense of the thousand acres, I guess. Are there other examples of this concept out there? Other experiences that might give us some indication of market demand. Though I may be way behind the curve on this one. You probably have budget numbers and assumptions that will clarify market questions."

"We're not approaching this project the same way we would a normal investment property," Bryan Thompson interjected, having said nothing to this point.

A mortgage banker with a very conservative approach to underwriting, Bryan had worked with me on several projects and had been the one on the phone the previous week with the invitation for this little plane ride. To hear him say what he just said was almost surreal. The small plane lurched up and down on some thermal currents as if recognizing a shift in the earth's rotation. All four passengers maintained steady eye contact without saying anything until the air and the stomachs settled. This included Lawrence Hill, another new name and face for me.

"Bryan I've known for years," I said when the plane steadied and our eyes loosened on one another, "so I can only assume that one of you has the Lord's ear, if only to make sure there's not an Icarus among us." An awkward silence followed, compelling me once again to cover my tracks. "I had a bad experience years ago, and small planes make me nervous."

"Not to worry, Mr. Felder," Richards replied reassuringly, "Eddie's been flying me around in this plane for a lot of years. Isn't that right, Eddie?" The pilot gave a thumbs up. Neither Eddie nor Dan Richards actually turned around to face each other. This was not their first rodeo.

"Must be one hell of a church for the preacher to have his own plane," I said.

Richards turned to look at Bryan, each nodding a conspiratorial nod before turning back to face me.

"Why do I get the feeling that you boys are connected and somebody's about to get tossed out of this thing?" I said, in surprisingly partial jest, at least to me.

"It's nothing like that, I assure you," he said with a chuckle. "I'm simply acknowledging Bryan's conformity to my request that this project retain a higher than normal level of secrecy."

"But you're not Mafia."

"Not even close."

"And you're not a preacher?"

"No more than we are all called to minister to others and spread the good word."

The plane achieved an uncannily smooth ride at about this time, so I sat back in my seat and tried to make the connections. Richards was quick to recognize my confusion.

"The easy answer is no," he said, "though I do feel a calling that guides my life and influences the activities of my daily business."

"And what business is that?"

"The automobile business. I have a couple of car lots."

This brought a chuckle from the others, though I was, once again, on the outside. Jason Sharp offered some clarification.

"More than a couple of car lots, I think," he said looking from Richards to me. "The Richards family controls franchises and dealerships across the Midwest. That's where the plane comes in handy."

"That makes sense," I nodded in affirmation. "And it reminds me of the old joke my grandfather used to tell about making a million bucks in the soybean business."

"How's that?" Lawrence Hill chimed in. Leave it to a preacher to perk up when somebody mentions an old anecdote or making a million dollars.

"By investing two million," Richards says, without taking his eyes off of mine. Hill got the joke, eventually. "So you think my vision is flawed?" Richards queried.

"Not my place to say," I replied, eye to eye. "Your money, your vision, your plane. I'm just happy to be here. Though," pausing for effect, "full disclosure, I am curious about why either one of us is up here, looking down there, thinking about building a temple to the Lord's amusement. Not judging, mind you. Just curious."

Richards looked back again to Bryan Thompson, and they shared another moment of unspoken understanding. That was one of the great parts of holding interested parties to a deal captive a couple thousand feet in the air. Like a conference room with a requisite chance of death. It serves to keep minds focused.

"I think we've seen enough, Eddie," Richards said, turning toward the cockpit as if he would need to turn the plane himself. "Let's head back to the barn." The plane banked left toward the airport and Richards turned back to face me."

"I like curious," he said, "and Bryan mentioned that you had an unconventional way of approaching developments from a philosophical perspective, a very creative bent, I think he said." His use of the third person in this instance was interesting, since Bryan was sitting no more than two feet to his right. "And that's what this project will need. That's why you're up here, looking down there, as you say. My interest in this project should be fairly obvious. I wear my faith on my sleeve. Always have and always will, as I think the Lord calls us to do. And while I appreciate your concern that this might be my soybean farm, rest assured that I undertake this project with the same critical eye I use in my business. That is to say I'm not blinded by my faith."

I felt as if I should assure him that I would never make such an assumption, especially since I seemed to be getting something of a scolding, but the better part of me rose to silence, affirming my supposition that I was just along for the ride and remained clueless as to why I was along for the ride. This last part he seemed to understand.

"As for your role, let me be clear. We will need some unconventional thinking to make this work, as I mentioned, and you've had some real history with that, from what I understand, actual experience developing retail spaces that are conceptually unique and compelling. Strip malls that tell a story, if you will."

"That may be," I replied with a cursory glance in Bryan's direction, "and I'm flattered by your assessment of my work, but you're not talking about a retail space."

"Am I not?" he replied simply and without hesitation.

"I didn't think so. But even if you are, I'm definitely the wrong guy to be building a retail experience—or anything else for that matter—around God."

"Are you not?" he replied again without hesitation.

"Well, we just met, so I can't help but wonder what makes you think that?"

The little light above the seats came on with a pleasant tone, signaling that the plane was about to land. Richards led the small group in the strange ballet of fastening seat belts and preparing for landing before turning back to me.

"Well you did go to seminary, didn't you? Back in the 80's?"

The raised eyebrows gave witness to my surprise and to Bryan's, as our eyes met quickly, mine wondering why he would've shared that information until his revealed that my tour of duty in the Lord's Army was news to him.

"I like to know who's riding on my airplane," he continued.

"I guess you do," I replied with a nod of affirmation, "but that was a lifetime ago in a place far, far away."

"Funny thing about seminary," he said, looking out the window to watch the ground rising beneath us, "the experience either fortifies your faith or sends you running for the hills of reason." While I agreed at first blush, I said nothing. "For our purposes, though, your spiritual journey is irrelevant. I'm not paying the would-be preacher. We got enough of those on board as it is." My eyes involuntarily shot to Lawrence Hill who, fortunately, was also watching the ground beneath our wings, oblivious to the reference. "I'm paying for the curiosity. No matter where you stand on the big questions, you continue to drink from the seminary well, working to prove or disprove your inclinations, as Satan reminds you of the artificial suspension of free will and the Holy Spirit extends the timeless invitation of redemption."

I watched his face in profile, as he stared out the window, and all I could think was that the rhetoric was either really advanced for a businessman or the crafted spiel of a car salesman. Either way, when we touched down, he turned for the closing.

"Make it your own," he said, "a reflection of your struggle. That's where the project will find solid ground. I'll worry about the money. Bryan will work out the financing. Jason will grease the wheels. Lawrence will tie us to the religious establishment. And you will create a space that tells a story. Perhaps the greatest story ever told."

"Yeah, but --"

"And the people will come, and they will pay, pray, and replay the experience for their friends and family, spreading the good news and God's message of hope and redemption. Our story. The story you create that converts that land into a wholly new place. And that's what you're being called to do. Welcome aboard."

Within what seemed like minutes, I was standing with Bryan on the tarmac outside Charlotte's general aviation terminal watching Eddie go wheels up to make one final loop over the site before continuing on to Cincinnati with Sharp, Hill, and Richards.

"What the fuck was that?" I asked Bryan, understating my confusion.

"That, my friend, was crazy money in the throes of realized mortality."

"Is he serious?"

"Very. So is his balance sheet. Both mean business, and that means business for you and me both. So get back in your car and get in touch with that part of you that keeps whining about writing a novel. This is your blank page."

"Not exactly what I had in mind."

"Maybe not, but I know your mortgage banker. Start driving and start dreaming."

Later That Night

Sherman, Georgia. The ironic suburb of Atlanta that a generation ago had been nothing more than a crossroads on the way to Athens, the intersection of agriculture and rabid football fans speeding backwards from adult responsibilities to their college memories and frat houses for a 24-hour respite from reality. Time's march to the sea had blazed an eight-lane concrete trail through Sherman over the last thirty years, sparing no pasture or woodland, forcing spec houses and strip malls into every nook and cranny and eradicating all indigenous fauna and flora while retaining their spirit in the beautifully landscaped stone gateways and evocative, marketable community names like Quail Ridge, Pine Hollow, Deer Woods, Mallard Cove, and Mountain Oaks.

I am not so much immune to the proliferation of commercial sprawl as responsible for it, a thought that had long-since left my consciousness until today, when my perspective on the entrance gates and guard hut for Cypress Valley bears the weight of the morning flight and occupational challenge. Or calling, as Dan Richards had said. I slow and consider the gates anew, the hut guard-less as always. This can't be all of me. It was a fleeting thought, and it came and went in the same instance, ushered ahead by a series of honks from the large SUV behind me, pushing me into the gated community we both called home.

Walking into the kitchen from the garage, I met only the remaining oxygen in the room, itself looking to the door as a likely way out. The setting sun filtered through the breakfast room sheers and cut a sharp angle on the small box on the table. Dropping my keys and phone on the edge of the kitchen counter, I walked over to the table to read the small note taped to the box. At the top she had written "Thib" in big letters. Below that, in smaller letters, "Casserole in fridge. Late match. Home after." In the box was a collection of catalogs and credit card offers along with a few bills and envelopes that looked legitimate. I looked from the box to the refrigerator, picked up the box, and decided that dinner with my younger brother was more inviting than cold casserole. Sweeping my arm across the kitchen counter to grab my keys and phone, I thought briefly about calling first. My brother seemed to be in a constant state of transition, though, and I had to get back in the car to eat anyway. I closed the door and keyed the deadbolt.

Pulling into the Interstate Climate Storage after business hours, I fished a card from behind my visor and read the codes, remembering that it had been almost a month since I'd seen my brother and that there was no guarantee that he would even still be in town. Walking through the aluminum-clad hallways and polished concrete floors beneath the hum of dehumidifiers, the lights illuminating the path only after the motion sensors determined that it was necessary, I followed the maze until reaching D423, a 10x20 unit leased by Thibodeaux Felder on a month-to-month lease to store his life while in transition. The lock was missing, though the rolling door was closed. The office had not locked him out of the unit, nor would they as long as my credit card remained valid.

I pulled the rolling door up and looked around the small space, confused by the idea that my brother would be so careless. A fully assembled double bed was pushed up against the left wall, framed by a wall of boxes to the rear, a low dresser on the wall opposite the foot of the bed, a duffle bag on top spilling clothes. Next to the head of the bed was a makeshift table of boxes. On the table a recent Chinese take-out meal sat with empty beer can bookends and a paperback Nietzsche. I could only shake my head in disbelief.

In the distance I heard footsteps. They made their way through the maze and appeared to be heading in my direction, undoubtedly my brother, though at times he appeared to have more than two feet. As the sounds drew closer, he also seemed to be talking, to himself or someone else. I couldn't tell, and I was frozen in place until he turned the corner with a young woman in tow. Our eyes met and a big grin came across his face.

"What did I tell you, Calliope," he said without hesitation, "Big Brother is always watching." The young woman rolled her eyes and pushed him away, obviously punctuating a joke I hadn't been privy to.

"I was talking about the security cameras, smart ass," she replied, and then she turned to look at me, trying to fit me into the puzzle she'd been working on as long as she'd known my brother, a time period that might've been anywhere from hours to years, though I couldn't remember meeting her or hearing her name.

"Hello, big brother," Thib offered, both in greeting and explanation. "What brings you to this neighborhood?"

"Brought the mail," I replied. "Thought you might like some dinner. But it seems like you've already got plans." I tossed the box of mail into the unit and turned back to him. "Nice digs."

"Wait," the young woman interjected, "you've got a brother? I thought you said you were homeless and an only child."

"Thanks," he said to me. "It's functional, but far from ideal. It suits my budget."

"It does have a certain economy to it."

"Calliope," he said, eyes still smiling toward me, "meet my uber-successful big brother, Chad Felder the Capitalist, developer to the kings."

"And spontaneous spoiler of plans," I said with a smile, "so I'll leave you two to face the evening as you had envisioned it."

"Not because of me, I hope," Calliope said quickly. "I'm late for work already, though Tuesday nights never really amount to much anyway."

There was an awkward pause as Calliope recovered her purse from its unseen perch behind some boxes and returned to give Thib a kiss on the cheek.

"We'll talk tomorrow," she said to him with a smile and, turning to me, "it was nice meeting you. Enjoy your dinner." She turned and began her exit through the maze, and only then did I notice the upper lines of her lower back tattoo, framed by the intersection of the white thong escaping from the top of her low-rise jeans. As she turned the first corner, and as if she knew with the confidence of an experienced young woman that we would both be watching her walk away, she turned and gave us a parting glance. I couldn't tell for sure, but I think I saw an invitation in that glance. For both of us.

Although we immediately turned to each other to acknowledge that we'd both been busted, we allowed time for her to walk to the elevator before resuming the conversation.

"So how long have you and Calliope been shacking up at the storehouse?" I asked with a gesture toward the storage unit.

"Shacking up may be a stretch," Thib replied, making his way into the unit as if looking for something. His wallet? Watch? Keys? It was tough to say for sure since the lights in the neighboring section had turned off from lack of motion. "We met a couple of weeks ago. She tends bar at a jazz and blues club over in the Highlands." He stood on a small stool I hadn't noticed and waved his hands near the ceiling, apparently reaching a motion sensor and reactivating the lights above and behind the unit. It appeared that the stool had been placed there for that purpose. "She lives over in that area too, off of Briarcliff, with her folks and her kid."

"Well, I hope she sees this for the gravy train that it really is," I asserted. "Her folks know she's got a Sugar Daddy with a storage unit outside the perimeter?"

"Relax. It's not like that."

"Oh, I get it. You sit around the storage unit and read Nietzsche to each other, and take turns clapping the lights on and off. Pretty fucking cerebral, if you ask me."

Thib seemed to give up looking for whatever he'd been hunting and turned slowly to look at me with a confused expression on his face, though framed in the cool, hipster countenance characteristic of someone comfortable enough in his own skin to set up house in a storage unit and shamelessly entertain there.

"Who shoved a reindeer up your ass, my brother?" he asked with his trademark sincere concern and a twist of urban slang. "If I was new to the fuck-up business, I might expect this rain of judgment, but I achieved veteran status years ago. You know that. So this ain't about me. You want to come clean or you want to carry this baggage all the way through dinner? Cause I heard something about you buying me dinner, and this line of bullshit ain't much of an appetizer." And then, out of the corner of his eye, he caught sight of his keys and retrieved them, turning back to me with raised brow and cock of the jaw looking for an answer.

"Let's get some food," I replied with a shrug. "You're right. This is not about you. And you are a veteran fuck-up. But then, I have an empty four-bedroom house in the suburbs and my little brother lives in a storage unit, so maybe there's enough of that to go around."

"Don't summon the guilt and then try to own my choices, friend. This is my life. Granted, technically it's your storage unit, but it's my life." He pulled the rolling door down and locked it. "And besides," he continued with a nod after Calliope, "you can't nail that sweetness in the suburbs. She likes the edge."

"A storage unit?"

"I know. Sick isn't it? But she really digs it for some reason. Like keeping a vibrator in the closet, I guess. But it works for me."

We walked to the elevators and made our way to the lobby and loading area, past the push carts and into the Atlanta night. I was still trying to get my mind around Calliope's interest in climate-controlled sex when Thib mumbled low beneath his breath, apparently spotting seconds ahead of me the three men leaning back against the trunk of a long, low-slung Mercedes. I made a connection only after they had begun walking toward us and Thib straightened his posture as if readying for a blow.

"Boudreaux," boomed a voice from the group. "Something told me you'd be laid up with that piece of fine that just left," he continued, walking toward us flanked on either side. "My boys here tell me she walked in there a couple hours ago with nothing and I watched her walk back out just now with nothing but a smile. I don't even want to know 'bout that. You rich white folks do some crazy ass shit."

"Not as crazy as you might imagine, Jeremiah."

I was confused by this exchange because the men standing menacingly before us were also white. The leader, Jeremiah, was flanked by two goons who must've played football until all eligibility expired. While the man in the middle wore a tailored suit and neatly trimmed hair, the security detail appeared more like ten pounds of sugar in five-pound bags, and they wore wraparound shades beneath closely-cropped buzz cuts.

"Who's Tom Brokaw over here?" Jeremiah asked, looking at me but still talking to Thib.

"That's my brother. He's taking me to dinner."

I still hadn't made any progress connecting these guys with Thib, and short that connection I defaulted to a middle-aged suburban male response to confrontation: calm, cool, and collectedly wide-eyed and silent.

"Well," Jeremiah drew out his response, "ain't that just the picture of brotherly love." He turned back to Thib and continued, "But what about this brother?

You got any love for me, my brother? Cause it seems I'm due. Would you agree?"

Thib nodded in the affirmative and started to put together a response, but I could tell his defining shuck and jive wasn't effervescing as it normally did. My protection instinct kicked in and I dove in for the save.

"I don't know anything about all this," I said with all the negotiation skill I could muster, "but --"

The hand appeared from nowhere at the end of Jeremiah's extended arm and punctuated my sentence effectively. His eyes never left Thib's and his tone was decidedly calm.

"When I want the news, Tom Brokaw, I'll fucking let you know. Now back to you, Boudreaux. What's the forecast call for today. We talking sunshine or am I gonna cloud up and rain all over this motherfucker?"

I didn't know whether to be concerned or humored. Jeremiah seemed at first to be almost a caricature of a gangster, a young white male speaking with the hip urban slang of society's underbelly. He had extreme confidence, though, and he held the beef brothers on a tight leash, so I determined my best strategy was to let Thib work through whatever issues this guy had.

"It's all sun, Jeremiah," Thib replied with enthusiasm, "all sun. But I need a couple days to make a clean transaction. Otherwise it gets stormy for you and me both."

Jeremiah seemed to consider this with the same calm, expressionless face for a really long time. He lowered his arm and I felt relieved, though I didn't know why.

"But you agree that I'm due?" he said.

"I do," Thib said with a nod.

"And that now you're on my time. Your time is out, you see. Now you're on my time, and I don't like to waste my time. We clear on that?"

"Yep."

"Okay. Just so we understand one another. If I don't have complete satisfaction in 48, the boys here will be back to get all cajun hillbilly on your ass, Boudreaux. Don't waste my time."

With that he turned, shooting me a purposeful glance, and walked back to his car. He climbed into the back seat, cell phone to his ear, while his entourage took the front, and easily the strangest part of my really strange day slid out of the parking lot and into the hectic stream of commerce that is Atlanta traffic. I felt like my feet had melted into the hot asphalt of the parking lot. I hadn't been able to move even as Thib had already made it to my car and was waiting by the passenger door with calm impatience.

"Ready?" he asked. "I'm starving."

"What the fuck?" was all I could muster, wide-eyed and almost literally beside myself. "I'm accosted in a parking lot because of your dumb ass, and all you can think about is food?"

"Well, you did offer dinner."

"Does none of this register with you, or are you so removed into your groovy, off the grid, pin the tail on the barmaid life that you failed to see the threat in whatever he was talking about? Is this just another Tuesday for you," I continued, now finding my feet and beginning to make my way to the car, "because I can't say the same. Jesus Christ, what the hell have you gotten into? Never mind. Don't answer that."

"Don't be so dramatic. Jeremiah likes to play gangster. We go way back."

"Yeah, I got the feeling you two were tight."

We didn't say anything for a while. I started the car and pointed it in the direction of a chain steak house, my car feeling the gravitational pull back into the world as I knew it, instead of the really bad reality TV show of the last half hour. The interstate was busy as darkness descended and the orange of the mercury vapor lights beat a steady 70-mph beat across the windshield. After my pulse normalized, I tried to get a handle on this latest live wire that had my brother by the short hairs.

"You're not playing this one off, Thib. If that thug comes back and pops a cork in your ass, I'm guilty too."

"Cap."

"What?"

"Pops a CAP in my ass, you suburban oenophile. Get your urban slang right before you assume responsibility for my underworld death."

"Whatever. You know what I mean. I'm not trying to own your life. I was just trying to deliver the mail and feed you a meal."

"That part sounds good."

"You seem to take this all in stride. You trying to tell me not to worry about any of this?"

"Exactly what I'm trying to say."

Even Later That Night

"And then he said the strangest thing," I said, taking the tie from around my neck and recounting the evening's events.

"Anything he could say at this point would've seemed strange to me," my wife said, looking over the top of her book and reaching for her wine glass on the bedside table. Though we had married late and only four years before, Molly had grown accustomed to my trials and tribulations with my brother, and even the part about the goons in the parking lot had come as no great shock. Hardly registered a pause from her intense consideration of the latest book club selection.

"He said, 'Fear not the jackal in plain view. It's the one you can't see.' Right as we got back to the place he's staying."

"Where's that?"

"Over by Highlands with some twenty-something." She seemed interested in his living situation, but I thought it best to conceal the actual situation. While unlikely, Molly might've suggested Thib move into our house temporarily if she had known about the storage unit.

"Typical. Sounds like more of his psychobabble. Probably whatever the latest hippy spiritual crap he read."

"Maybe," I said, walking into the closet to find a hanger for the suit I was happily removing after too many hours of service. "But I think there's more to it than that."

"What makes you say that," she replied without looking up.

"The only place I've ever read that was on my mother's suicide note."

Molly let the book fall to the comforter and looked up just as I was coming out of the closet and walking toward the bathroom. I had anticipated that this would pique her interest, and I was right. Our eyes met as she was trying to reconcile the stories of our courtship.

"I thought you said your mother died when you were very young."

"She did. I think I was eleven and Thib was six or seven."

"Pretty important detail to leave out, don't you think?" she said, elbowing up on her pillows to get a better view of my response.

"Long time ago in a place far, far away." By this point I was in the bathroom working toothpaste onto the brush and contemplating just how far we were going to drill down on this topic. In my defense, I'm not aware of any time that Molly had asked about the specifics of my mother's death, and I had always quietly maintained that she died when I was young, suggesting perhaps that the details had always been ahead of me. I considered brushing that line of rhetoric back into my mouth, along with the cleansing fluoride, but she was leveraging the linens for a talk, and that rarely worked in my favor.

"What happened?"

"Daddy always said she faced down some demons, especially after Janine was killed." I tried to slide the last part of that into the equation, recognizing that we had talked about Janine at least once, looking through some old family albums very early in our marriage, probably when we were moving into the house, but not wanting to introduce the possible connection between the events into the conversation and thereby expanding my own negligence and guilt.

"And she left a note?"

"Yep."

"And you think Thib brought that expression up out of thin air as a way of saying he's suicidal?"

"Not really," I replied without much hesitation. "Never figured him for the type. Mother was manic depressive. If Thib faced the same demons, the doctors say he would've been fighting them hard by his mid-twenties. I mean, he's got his demons, but I don't think they're violent. But that's not the strange part."

"What is the strange part?"

"He never saw the note."

"What, you mean your mother's note?"

"Yep." I had pulled back the covers on my side of the king bed and was climbing in. "He was only six or seven and couldn't really read, so Daddy never showed it to him. Didn't want to scare him with some story about jackals and shit like that, I guess."

"But he showed it to you?"

"Actually, I showed it to him."

"I don't understand," she said, rolling onto her side and resting on her elbow, looking at me looking at the ceiling.

"I walked home from school that day just like always, and when I got to our street Daddy was leaning against his car along the curb in front of the house. I assumed he was waiting for me, so I started running down the block on the sidewalk until I saw the ambulance in the driveway, lights still spinning on the top. That stopped me cold, but it didn't scare me. I knew what was going on, and he knew I knew.

He met me in the middle and we walked back around the block the other way, ambulance fading behind us as he shared the general series of events, ending with her swallowing a bottle of pills and making the last minute call to him."

"Damn," she said almost under her breath. Eerily similar to the morning response to a related story, but I wasn't going there.

"So we got in the car and headed off to pick up Thib from school," I continued, retelling the story almost as dispassionately as I would read a menu, having played this tape a million times in my mind. "I asked Daddy if a jackal was something we should be afraid of and said he didn't think so, not in South Georgia. Why, he asked, and I opened my lunch box and handed him the note that Mama had put in with my lunch that day. 'Fear not the jackal in plain view. It's the one you can't see.'

"In your lunch box? What did he do?"

"That's when he first talked about her demons, and he asked if he could hold on to the note for a while, and he said we probably shouldn't mention it to Thib. So I never did."

"And that was it?"

"Yep. We cremated her and spread her ashes along the beach down near Alligator Point, just like she wanted, though I don't think that last part was legal. I've never really been a fan of the beach since then."

This drew a frustrated chuckle out of Molly, though her facial expression had little room for levity.

"Why have you never told me any of this? It had to be pretty traumatic for an eleven-year-old boy to carry his mother's suicide note in his lunch box. That's really twisted."

"Like I said," turning from the ceiling to her, pushing the point home, "long time ago in a place far, far away. I didn't even think about the note again until I graduated from seminary. Daddy had given me a leather-bound bible to mark the occasion, even though he was never really religious. I assumed it was his way of starting a family Bible. Inside was the jackal note with a copy of the obituary and a letter from him reminding me of the power of forgiveness and suggesting that, one day, I would want to have a conversation with Thib about all of that."

"And did you?"

"Not yet, but it's on my list. Daddy had a stroke and died about six years later. I kept the note in there to remind me, but I never got to it. And then Thib fled the reservation, so there's that."

"Was he ever really on the reservation?"

"Good point," I replied with a yawn, reaching up to turn out the light on the bedside table.

Later that night, after surrendering to Molly's snoring and my own bladder's appeal for relief, I migrated to my office above the garage, in what was originally a bonus room, to unload the road behind and speculate on the road ahead. I scrolled through emails looking for fires and then tried to capture the essence of the Charlotte project to begin the creative process. Would a God experience be more of an amazement park than an amusement park? Weak, but it was 3:00 a.m. What did I expect? Dan Richards had said the project would take me back to my seminary days, so I shuffled over to the closet in search of the remnants. On a top shelf, way back in the farthest corner of the closet, was a box labeled "Seminary." One box. What had been my calling, my certain path to understanding the world and making a difference in it had been reduced to one box, shoved as far back into the dusty corners of my life as possible. And it was a light box at that. I didn't hold out much hope for great revelations to move the Charlotte project along. I took the box back to the folding plastic table I used for a desk—a temporary furnishing that had achieved semi-permanent status—and rifled through the contents.

I was honestly amazed that the box wasn't lighter, having trouble imagining why I had saved any of the stuff. Near the bottom of the box was the Bible my father had given me for graduation. I pulled it out and considered it carefully, almost spooked by its presence there considering the day's events and conversations, before finally admitting the possibility that it was what I came looking for in the first place. At least what was stashed inside of it. Or supposed to be. I thumbed through the whole book several times, but the note was not to be found. I dug around in the bottom of the box but didn't find it there either. I walked back over to the closet to see if there was a second, smaller box that I simply hadn't seen before, but there wasn't. Not much to do about it now, I consoled myself, but I still needed to have the conversation with Thib. Sure would help to have the point of the conversation in hand, though.

I heard sounds coming from the main part of the house and looked up expecting to see Molly walk in squinty-eyed to make sure I was okay. That's probably how it would've played out in a book or a movie, but that wasn't Molly's schtick. She snored the wine-induced slumber of the innocent, the emotionally disconnected, the comfortably numb. The ticking sounds were actually coming from the steam generator above our shower, and I was reminded that Irving was expecting me to research the repair options. God created the world in seven days but he couldn't create a steam shower worth a shit. And for this we should build Him an amusement park? As I eased back into the bed—yeah, like she was going to wake up—the strangeness of the day pulled my entire body into the mattress beneath me and I was motionless, heavy with the gravity of the events in motion. I was still. I listened. All I heard was the ticking. And the snoring.

August 12

    I woke with a start, a jolt that threw my neck into a building web of cramps. It was the gun shot that did it, though in my waking haze I couldn't figure out whether fight or flight was the appropriate response. Fortunately, my bedroom was completely free of thugs and gangsters, though their absence only made it more difficult to assess the urgency of the situation. I held the back of my neck as I scanned the room. The only light entered the room from the windows, poorly draped in expensive fabric. The door to the bathroom and closets beyond was open. The elliptical machine in the corner was characteristically free of towels and dirty clothes. Obsessive compulsive behavior had lately emerged as one of Molly's more charming attributes. Her attention to exercise and laundry—and the potential confluence thereof—was awe inspiring, especially when her use of the machine was essentially a warm-up act for her regular workout routines that rarely began or ended at Ultimate Fitness, her gym. Well, our gym. We had a family membership, though I hadn't darkened the door in several months, which probably enhanced her substantial popularity among the other patrons, especially the males.
    This flash of recollection, however, did nothing to bring the smoking gun into clearer focus, for nothing in the room seemed visually out of place. Then small sounds began creeping into the darkness, all part of the flow of light from the other side of the windows. Muted by double-pane glass, the sound of engines came through more as a hum than a roar, reminding me that no fewer than a half dozen hispanic laborers of mixed legality had descended upon my half acre

wielding walk-behinds and weed whackers in pursuit of the American dream. This firm footing in the reality of Wednesday calmed my neck cramps, as did the sharp clap of the mower backfiring as it passed beneath the window. I had to smile groggily at the thought of thugs, until the night before danced back into my vision, reminding me of the dream that had been interrupted by the gunshot.

Wanting to leave the early morning behind me as quickly and efficiently as possible, I rose quickly, showered, and waved an appreciative and multilingual goodbye to the Landscape Solutions team. Driving through the neighborhood, once a haven for the Landscape Solutions of the world, I was reminded of one of the lesser economic indicators. I noticed that an increasing number of my neighbors, most not much older than me, were spending the early part of their workday saddled up on their new Craftsman or John Deere mowers, DINKs now OINKs, and whatever the equivalent would be for those with kids. I was reminded of my father's spin on yard work, probably meant to contain young boys with more energy than sense. He called yard work urban agriculture and insisted that it connected us to our rural roots. Somehow my neighbors seemed ill-suited to urban agriculture and appeared almost naked without the protection of a tie and a European sedan. In the rearview mirror, a collection of several mowing neighbors in view appeared to dance a strange ballet of close turn radiuses and crosshatch patterning.

Another economic indicator was the staff that greeted me when I reached the office. Never a fan of corporate office buildings and completely unable to reconcile cubicles with creativity, I hung out my own shingle fairly early in my development career, and that shingle now hung on another of my early ideas, an office cooperative. I converted an old warehouse into office suites, lofty subdivisions now occupied by architects, ad men and women, a couple of lawyers with a creative bent, and several lone ranger practitioners like myself who had no staff and could expect no greeting, other than Mildred's smile and extended hand clutching a bouquet of pink "While You Were Out" message flowers. Mildred was a shared resource, but she shared sparingly, even with me. Mildred had been with the project from the beginning and managed the whole affair with a stern attention to detail and a redhead's inability to suffer fools.

The co-op had been an idealistic venture from inception, drawing creative minds into a common space to allow for the possibility of spillover, the chance that a lawyer with a love for architecture or an architect enduring litigation might mention in passing a nugget of truth valuable only to the hearer, a perspective that could conceivably change the course of a development project or help an insurance salesman demonstrate sufficient empathy to close the next sale. Or, at the very least, the hope that conversations in the common spaces might stray from normal occupational discourse to include the arts, big ideas, evolving philosophies. The reality included more sports and talk radio than I'd had in mind, but it really didn't matter since I spent very little time in the office anyway. The project had succeeded in allowing me to bring in old friends who could appreciate the creative concept, and one of those friends was Randy Wilkerson, an architect whose work I admired and opinion I valued, even when there were no buildings involved.

"Randy in?" I asked Mildred, who had not yet looked up from her People Magazine but could clearly see the blinking phone bank.

"On the other line. Would you like to leave a message?"

"No, but thanks," I replied with a smile.

"Suit yourself."

I made my way through the open spaces of the building, past the reception seating area, the conference room, the rest rooms and break area, before climbing the single flight of cantilevered stairs to the mezzanine floor above. The upper offices were encased largely in glass with contemporary lighting and finishes. I passed Randy's office on the way to my own and saw that he was in the process of hanging up his phone. I wheeled around and stuck my head in his door.

"Got a therapeutic moment?"

"Your couch or mine?" was his reply, though neither office had a couch, or a therapist for that matter.

"Mine," I replied, holding up Mildred's bouquet of pink message slips. "It will give me an excuse to not return these calls for a little longer."

Randy walked in my office less than a minute behind me, closed the door, sat down and threw his feet up on my desk, laced his fingers behind his head and cleared his throat.

"Waitress or lonely road vixen?" he asked.

"What?"

"You called me in here for absolution," he replied without emotion. "I'm just cutting to the chase."

"Hotel clerk," I replied with mock indignation, "but that's not the point."

"Okay. What is the point?"

"I had a really fucked up dream."

"Red meat and too much wine. You have dessert? Could be reflux."

"It's not reflux, moron. Just listen."

"I'm all ears, except for that moron part. Remember you called me in here. I got buildings down the hall that need my attention. Shithead."

"Right. Good comeback. The trick is, part of this dream was actually real, like it was pulling from a highlights reel from my childhood and mixing in some other stuff from I don't know where."

"And you want me to plug the Freud in?"

I stopped and stared, as if I expected Randy to hold forth on the interpretation of dreams and there was little I could do to stop him.

"Fire away," he said.

"I was very young, and I was asleep in my childhood bed, part of a set centered around a sailor motif with anchors on the headboards. In the bed next to me, Thib slept with a blanket twisted around his fist, a habit he'd actually returned to after Janine's death. I told you about that, didn't I? The Grand Canyon?"

"Yep."

"Anyway, it was early on a school day, and Daddy was shaking us awake and encouraging us both to rise and shine, gathering our shoes and books and almost carrying us out the front door of the house and into the warm, idling car in the driveway. In the dream it seemed funny that my father was waking us up. That was something my mother always did. I assume mothers did that sort of thing, at least up until the women's rights thing came along."

"Tick tock."

"Right. But that morning, in the dream, my father woke us up and got us dressed and drove us to school." Here I paused just long enough to allow Randy a foot in the door.

"That's it? That's the whole dream? Jesus, Felder, you have got to be kidding me. Hell, even red meat and wine couldn't choke up that drivel. My kids have better visions than that."

"Not done yet. Hold up. That part actually happened. I remember it."

"Thrilling. Really captivating so far."

"Then there was this bright flashing light as we're pulling out of the driveway, a confusion of colors that seemed to gather in the lower tree limbs that hung out over the driveway and the road. In the dream, it was like Joseph in his dream coat, a sign from God that I was among his favorites and that my life would be the envy of my brothers."

"You got more than one?"

"Metaphorically, asshole."

"Do us both a favor and skip ahead to the good part."

"In the dream I rise through the bands of color and through the trees and come to rest on a cloud, like a fluffy white recliner, just inside the pearly gates, and just like the pictures on the funeral home fans, there's Jesus or Saint Peter or somebody, calling roll."

"Are you skipping ahead?"

"So my family starts to arrive behind me. Father, brother, mother, all arriving at roughly the same time and being greeted at the gates. But when Saint Peter checks the roll, he shakes his head."

"Southbound. Damn shame."

"Then he pulls out a big gun and puts it at my mother's head and looks at me, and for the first time I notice that the hand holding the gun is black, even though his face is as white as his flowing robes."

Randy just stares at me and says nothing, so I continue.

"He raises his eyebrows as if he's asking me what I want to do, like it's my decision whether my mother lives or dies, whether my family lives or dies, since they're all bunched together and separate from me. And the three of them look to me as well, though their expressions are serene, almost oblivious to the fact that there's a big gun to their heads. And then Saint Peter mouths the question, 'What's it gonna be, white boy?' Which seems odd coming from a white face draped in white robes."

"Tell me you pulled a 9 mil and popped a cap in Saint Pete's ass!"

"I didn't know how to respond or even who or what to respond to, and the gunshot woke me up."

"So he shot her?"

"Well, actually it was a mower that backfired, so I don't know if he shot her or not."

Randy seemed confused by the addition of a lawn mower, and I thought I should spare him the details.

"That was it, really. It got confused there at the end, but my question to you is why, at this point in my life, would I remember an event in my life differently and confuse the actual details with a message from God?"

"Am I to assume you'd be open to a message from God? I thought you gave that up years ago."

"Well, the obvious connection involves a new project in Charlotte, a theme park of sorts, where God operates the concession stand and makes the merry go round and round. I was up there yesterday for the initial site visit and the money behind the project is old school New Testament."

"Sort of like a Jesusland?"

"Sort of, but I'm sliding down from the tip of the iceberg at this point. And I was up late going through an old box of seminary stuff trying to generate some ideas, but that wheel ain't been greased in a long time."

"What details were different?"

"About seminary?"

"No. About the dream. You said you confused the actual details with the dream. Do you remember the details?"

"Yeah. I remember the lights flashing up in the tree limbs and reflecting in the rearview mirror."

"Sign from God?"

"No. It was an ambulance. Paramedics were pulling in the driveway as we were pulling out."

"What?"

"Yeah. Turns out my mother wasn't able to get past Janine's death. She swallowed a bunch of pills. The first of two tries. And Daddy took us to school that day."

There was a silence bridging the two of us, though Randy and I could both hear the outside world. He knew better than to question the details or mock their revelation, having heard most of the other of my family dramas by this point. He could only shake his head as he stared at his feet, still propped on my desk, eyes moving slowly back and forth like his toes were playing tennis.

"Why do you tell me all this shit and why do I still listen?

"But do you think the dream is trying to tell me something?"

"Hell if I know, but I'll tell you this much. You got some serious haints in that noggin of yours, and you need more therapy than I'm licensed to provide, my friend. Don't tell that pretty wife of yours any of this shit or you'll be dividing up your worldly possessions a second time. And that would probably make her my landlord."

Randy dropped his feet to the floor in punctuation, put his hands on his knees preparing to rise, and looked me in the eye with an uncharacteristic expression of sincerity. He had formed his words but somewhere his mind was calculating their impact and running risk/reward scenarios before turning his mouth loose.

"You know where I stand on the supernatural, so I'm the wrong tree for all that barking. My hunch is that all this is part of the new project you picked up and you need to unpack all of that baggage before you go kneeling at the foot of any crosses."

There was a crisp knock at the glass door of my office and we both turned to see Randy's draftsman holding a cell phone up to the door. We turned back to face each other and he pushed himself to a standing position.

"And seriously, get some help with this history of yours, Felder. I know we're grown men and there's nothing you can do about the past and time marches on and all that, but you seem to have reached critical mass on being screwed up. I mean, I thought my in-laws were crazy, and they might be, but you are like the Warren Buffett of crazy past. You own it, you've got more of it than anybody else, and you still live happily in your own private Omaha. Damnedest thing I've ever seen."

I smiled as he left, taking the phone from his draftsman and stepping into the next conversation as he moved down the mezzanine to his own office. I held off explaining the possible connections with the hand holding a gun, surely a leftover from the previous night. Despite my passive views on religion, it seemed unlikely that God would require a handgun to get my attention. What did catch my eye was the fourth flower in Mildred's pink "While You Were Out" bouquet, a message from the manager of Interstate Climate Storage from earlier that morning.

"Good Morning. Interstate Climate Storage. How can I lock up your stuff today?"

"Manager, please," I replied, the quirky tagline almost lost on me.

"Speaking. How can I help?" To say her voice was chirpy or cheery would be misleading, though it did come through the line with a fervent optimism.

"Chad Felder, returning your call from this morning."

"Yes, Mr. Felder. How are you this morning?"

"Just trying to make it to lunch. Yourself?"

"Fine. Just fine, thanks. I was calling about a security issue that might limit your access to your unit."

"A security issue?"

"Yes, but it's nothing serious, and it is only temporary."

"Well, I don't really access the unit all that often."

"We will be performing routine maintenance on the keypad system this afternoon, and probably replacing several of the entry modules."

"Really?"

"Yes sir. We made the decision on such short notice that I wasn't able to post the usual signage."

"So you're calling everybody?"

"No, no. That would take a lot longer than the actual maintenance. I'm calling those customers on your floor who have accessed their units in the last 72 hours or so."

"Why the short notice, and why my floor, if you don't mind me asking."

"Nothing to be alarmed about, let me assure you. We've received a report of inter-unit trespass, somebody accessing units from within the other units on the floor."

"No shit?"

"Unfortunately, yes. But the good news is that nothing has been reported missing, and we've isolated the activity to your floor, so we're taking some industry-recommended preventative measures. This type of thing happens all the time in other places, though this is the first report we've had in our facility. That's the reason for the short notice. Trying to nip it in the bud, as they say."

"Okay. Well, thanks for letting me know. I had no plans to move anything in or out today, so no problem on this end. I'm assuming passwords will remain the same."

"Yes they will, and all the work will be done by the end of the day today."

By the end of the short conversation, I had turned my desk chair around to face the large bank of windows overlooking the rear parking lot, spaces predictably occupied by the same cars driven by the employees inside the building, day after day. There was an almost zen quality to the predictability, like the lines left in the sand by a careful hand and rake. Whenever someone in the building traded cars, they almost always returned to the same spot, though spots had never been reserved or even numbered. As I was hanging up the phone, I noticed a new car in the lot, parked in a space near the dumpster, a spot that had never really drawn anyone's loyalty. Too far from the building and too close to the trash. But this car was remarkable not only because it sat in relative isolation, but because the tinted windows were slightly cracked and smoke was emerging in patterned exhalations.

Noon

By the time the clock struck lunch I was ready to be on the road. I stopped at Mildred's desk on the way out, assuming she'd be a great source of religious commentary. As I leaned over the chest-high counter surrounding her workspace, I took inventory of the collection and arrangement of the items on her desk. There between the crucifix and the framed wedding picture was the daily prayer calendar, a page-a-day discipline for the soul, a twelve-step program with 365 steps. More with leap year. Mildred was on the phone, so she didn't see me struggling to read today's prayer entry, something about turning the other cheek. She hung the phone up and ran an imaginary string from my eyes to the calendar, returning to my eyes with passive cynicism.

"I'll get you one of your own," Mildred offered, "if you'll take the time to read it. Might do you some good, bring back some old memories."

Despite the doubling of her salary and the annual bonuses, Mildred could never quite forgive me for tempting her away from her previous employer, a small church on a high-traffic corner on the going home side of the road, the side favored by large national drugstore chains. The preacher she worked for held firm to the historical roots of the small church until a generous relocation allowance was supplemented with a similarly generous though less public amount for the preacher's discretionary fund. That had been the first of many corners I developed for national chains and big box retailers as the small county road heading northeast out of Atlanta had swollen to six lanes, swallowing the past and the quaint without really pausing to chew, and Mildred blamed me for all of it.

"Are you suggesting that I don't have enough religion in my life, Mildred?"

"Who am I to preach, especially to the man who was supposed to be a preacher?"

"But fate has brought us together to this point, Mildred. Don't you see?" She was having nothing to do with my melodrama.

"Did you want something from me, or were you just stopping by on your way out?"

"I need you to give me some of that old-time religion."

She stared blankly back at me and used the cap end of her pen to scratch behind her right ear, eyebrows raised in expectation that I would come to the point, and quickly.

"And here's the funny part: I'm not even kidding."

Mildred and I had known each other a long time. Her expression never changed.

"So here's the deal. I need you to think back on all your Biblical memories, all the stories you'd have me remember more fondly, and pick the twelve you think would make the greatest impact at Six Flags."

"Not funny," she said, turning back to her phone as if willing it to ring until I left the building.

"But necessary for research purposes. The Lord is prepared to multiply loaves and fishes, and a car dealer in Ohio is bound and determined to pay for it."

Mildred could only shake the back of her head at me while thumbing through the messages a third time.

"In Charlotte? The meetings yesterday? The new project?"

"What has the Lord got to do with a strip mall?" she asked, turning back to face me with a furrowed brow and squinted eyes.

"Very little, I assure you, but the new project is not, as it turns out, a strip mall, and what it is has everything to do with the Lord and the twelve compelling stories you need to pick out for me," I replied, my voice devolving into a cross between a gameshow host and a televangelist, if there's a difference there. "For Mildred," rising to crescendo, "the two of us will be exploring the concept of Jesusland! Hallelujah! Can I get a witness?"

Crickets.

"Let me get this straight," she said. "You've been hired to develop a religious shopping center somewhere near Charlotte?"

"You're not that far off," I had to admit, "given the likelihood of gift shops at every turn, but the concept is not really a shopping experience. It's more like a religious experience."

"Like a church?"

"Trust me when I say that you're asking the same questions I was asking yesterday, but we are not designing a church."

"Sure sounds like it."

"Twelve stories?" I asked, trying to pique her interest and get out of the building. "Can you spend some time this afternoon and come up with a short list?"

"It's your time I'm wasting" she replied with final resignation.

"Great. Thanks. I'll be back."

Walking out the back door of the building, I gave a quick glance toward the dumpster and the car that had taken up residence there. Tinted windows, cracked at the top, were the only memorable feature. Everything else looked showroom ready, as far as I could tell from a split-second look in that direction, and it didn't really concern me until I pulled out of the parking lot and the tinted sedan followed me into the flow of traffic. Great. Just what I needed.

"What the fuck have you gotten into?" I said to nobody in the car.

"What are you talking about?" came the reply, my brother's voice through the car's speakers and the miracle of bluetooth technology.

"I wasn't going to make it any of my business, but now it looks like a couple of your thug buddies are following me in a tinted Lexus, and I decided that I really ought to know the particulars surrounding my untimely death and dismemberment."

"Don't be so dramatic, "Thib offered condescendingly.

"Easy for you to say, through the phone, sitting in some mini-warehouse while your brother becomes a statistic in gang-related violence because you got sideways with the mafia."

"You watch too much television."

I tried to carry the conversation while thumbing through the mental playbook for diversion and avoidance when being followed, and the first idea that came to light was simply to alter course a couple of times to confirm my suspicions. So I turned left off the highway onto a side street that bisected two phases of a tired commercial center. I circled in front of the dead grocery anchor on the right side of the division and slowed in front to pretend I was checking out the vacant space. The tinted Lexus pulled into the left parking lot and stopped in front of a Mani/Pedi salon, though nobody got out of the car. After a minute or so I pulled back into the flow of highway traffic and watched as the Lexus followed a close distance behind.

"Well, shit."

"What?"

"Still following me. I pulled into a parking lot and stopped, but this guy is hanging on. Lucy, you got some splainin' to do," I said in my best Ricky Ricardo.

"I got nothing. How do you know it involves me? Could be an angry husband."

"Or the same asshole that put a gun to my head about 12 hours ago and mistook me for a much older news anchor. My money's on the second."

The car continued to follow me as I wove in and out of traffic, and it seemed unlikely that diverting into another parking lot would yield a different result. With a traffic light and congested intersection approaching, I estimated the cars in the lanes in front of me and made a last-minute switch that forced the Lexus to slowly pull alongside me in the next lane, windows tinted and cracked at the top.

"Well, if they're out to kill me, they got a clear shot right now."

"What?" Thib was still confused.

"Right beside me, in the next lane. Still can't see through the windows."

"Nobody's trying to kill you."

As the light was changing and the turning lanes were crossing oncoming traffic, I stole one last glance at the passenger side of the Lexus, just as the tinted window slid down into the doorframe. When the window was fully open, a large face framed by wraparound shades turned slowly without expression to face me. A lesser man might've shit his pants, but I still had no idea what these goons wanted from Thib, or from me. I held his gaze until he disappeared through the intersection and I was pushed through the same by the honking from the cars behind me. I think I started breathing again shortly thereafter and resumed the interrogation of my brother.

"Well, I think we can safely rule out the angry husband option."

"Why is that?"

"You'll just have to take my word for it. These were the strong, silent types that had no interest in my boring suburban existence until last night, I can assure you. The guy stared a hole through me like he could off me without even the slightest hesitation."

"Off you? Where does that shit come from, Bro? You writing hip-hop lyrics now?"

"Your concern for my safety is noted, and I'll be sure to reciprocate when these bastards string you up for whatever you're hiding. Bro. I gotta bounce, as they say. Peace out, you shit-for-brains."

"Wait! What the...."

The bluetooth cut him off as I watched the Lexus disappear into the commercial horizon framed on both sides of the road by the latest lifestyle center, oddly named The Summit since the terrain was flat enough to offer a view of the Atlanta skyline on a clear day. Though not one of my designs, it was an inviting shopping center with more than the average attention paid to architectural detail and green space. I looked at the clock embedded in the dash of my Volvo and began working on an apology for my late arrival. Molly had little patience for tardiness other than her own, and she had reinforced that intolerance on the phone earlier that morning, when I called to confirm our lunch date at Wanda's, a bistro and coffee shop tucked into a small space beneath our fitness center. Wanda was something of a local hero, and she had been a part of our family for years. Molly and I ate breakfast or lunch with Wanda at least a couple of times a week, and Molly often started her day with coffee after her morning workout. I smiled at Wanda and crossed the small dining room to the table, our table, where Molly was busy thumbing something to someone on her phone.

"I ordered your black bean wrap," she said without looking up.

"Perfect, thanks," I replied without apology, though thoughtfully prepared. "Sell any houses this morning?"

Molly looked up from her phone with a mock-confused expression before returning to her phone. Whatever she was thumbing, it seemed important. I decided it was prudent to keep quiet while she finished, so I crossed my legs in the direction of the windows looking out over the parking lot and watched the fitness parade, the arrival of the needy, the departure of the sated, and the curious ministrations of an attractive blond in tight running gear acting as drill sergeant to a half-dozen middle-aged guys whose tired expressions gave way to their elation that a half naked young woman was just a riding crop away from complete fulfillment of their every fantasy. They were doing push ups and squats and running around the parking lot with exercise balls. She was whipping them into an unrequited sexual frenzy without breaking a sweat or making any effort to mask her enjoyment, at least when they were looking.

"You should give her class a try," Molly said when putting her phone down hadn't reined in my complete attention. "She'll whip you into shape."

"Round is a shape, my love." One of the great transparencies of a childless second marriage is the ever-presence of the divorce card, poised among the unspoken inferences with subliminal criticism. "You should give her class a try" becomes "You were thinner when we married" or "Lose the weight or lose me." While the same nagging is characteristic of a first marriage, the threshold for departure is much lower in a second. Been there, done that, and life's too short to wait around. Something like that, anyway. I'm looking at her and she's looking at me as we silently negotiate the hand we've been dealt. Thankfully, Wanda saves the day by bringing our plates. Like I said, local hero.

"Did the yard guys show up this morning?" Molly asked while arranging the sandwich and fruit on her plate. "I left a note for them to blow off the back patio. They skipped that part last week."

"They were there when I left, but I didn't look out back." The black bean wrap was compelling. "How was your morning?"

"Uneventful. Things have really slowed down on the residential side. Few listings and even less interest in the ones we have. Everybody seems to be sitting on the sidelines trying to figure out what's next. How about you? What was the Charlotte job?"

"You wouldn't believe me if I told you."

"Try me."

"Jesusland."

She looked up from the grilled vegetables trying desperately to un-pita themselves and cocked her head sideways, letting body language ask the question her full mouth couldn't.

"They want me to conceptualize a theme park, I think, though I'm still trying to get my head around it. Some sort of fundamentalist amusement venture, like a cross between Billy Graham and Walt Disney."

Molly's expression suggested that she didn't quite trust my explanation, like the idea was so ludicrous that even I couldn't pull it off. Then her face lit up with a revelation.

"Wait a minute! I read something about this somewhere, but the place they were talking about was in Kentucky or West Virginia, and there were going to be several phases of residential development around it and a golf course. But they made it sound more like a megachurch than an amusement park."

"Different group, I guess. These folks seem set on rides and gift shops and plenty of Jesus going around. They call it an experience."

"What does that mean?"

"Beats the hell out of me, but they seem to think I can figure it out for them."

Molly and I had similar views on the God question, but we had never really talked about it. Church hadn't been of interest to her since we married, at least as far as I knew, and I certainly wasn't going to push it. We had talked about my seminary time as a part of the background section of the courtship ritual, but it had never really come up again. Until now.

"Is this one of Bryan's projects?" she said, processing religion and grilled vegetables at the same time.

"Yep."

"Didn't you guys go to seminary together or something like that?"

"No," I replied with a chuckle, "though it would be easy to make that assumption if you spent much time with the two of us. He drinks the Kool-Aid. Always has. But I've always held his feet to the reason fire, so we've talked about God a lot through the years. He's one of those who just seems too bright to buy into it."

"So why would he bring you in to do something like this?"

"Maybe he's on a mission to bring me to the foot of the cross, and I can respect that."

"How can you respect that if you don't drink the Kool-Aid? Seems like it would just be a pain in the ass to deal with if you know you don't agree with each other."

"Well," I mumbled, working the last bites of black bean into the mix, "it's strange, but we're really good friends and if he firmly believes in all that Jesus stuff and sees my ignorance as life-threatening, how can he not keep pushing that agenda. And the same with my perspective. If I firmly believe that faith in a supernatural is misguided and dangerous, leaving a good friend in the cloud of dogma seems irresponsible, almost negligent. So we have this sort of unspoken but natural tension that enjoys no definitive answers."

The television on the wall over Molly's shoulder was tuned to CNN, and the screen was filled with images of bomb blasts and bloodied bodies. I took another long pull on the sweet tea in front of me and then turned to watch the last of the boot camp boys sweating enough to supply the fountain of youth, the blond grinning subtly.

Once back in the car and heading back to the office, I watched the rearview mirror closely, trying to find the Lexus in a haystack. While they didn't seem to be tailing me on the return trip, I couldn't help but wonder if they had made a note of my lunch destination. To quell my paranoia, I decided to give Bryan Thompson a call.

"Thought you'd want to know that your name came up at lunch with Molly," I said when he answered. "Hope the phone didn't ring in your backswing. I know how you hate when that happens."

"Why do all the pretty women bring my name up at lunch?"

"Probably because they want you to pick up the check, Big Money."

"Story of my life. I hope you defended me where you needed to."

"Took a bullet or two. Nothing you wouldn't do for me."

"How long you been married?"

"To this one?"

"Yep. The other one doesn't count. Mulligan on the first hole."

"Little over four years. Why?"

"Just curious," he replied. "Thinking about kids?"

"Nope. My gene pool is best drained when I'm done swimming. I'm the end of the grand old line of Felders, much to the dismay of the trailer parks and correctional facilities across South Georgia."

"Don't you have a brother?"

"Yeah, but he probably won't live long enough to father a child," I said with a chuckle. "He runs against the forces of nature."

"I thought you said he was really smart."

"He is," I agreed, "when he pulls his head out of his ass. He knows everything there is to know about computers and technology, but he lives almost completely off the grid."

"Well, to each his own. You playing today?" he asked, "or are you sitting by the fire refreshing your memory of Bible verses?"

"More of the latter, though not quite the way you describe it."

Bryan Thompson was new to golf, but I was thankful he'd taken it up, even if he'd done so under the auspices of stronger business development potential than big game hunting, his primary recreational passion. While our golf together was infrequent, it had been fun to watch his skills improve, even though mine remained static in the comfortably social client golf range. He was probably correct in his assumption that golf was a better networking tool than killing things, and he reminded me of this when he described the invitation.

"Sending the plane for you," he said. "Dust off your clubs."

"Wish I could go, but I gotta say no," I replied, "especially if you want this little project of yours to see the light of day in the near term."

"No is not an option. Besides, you get to write it off, because it's wrapped around that little project of ours."

"How's that?"

"Dan Richards is our host," he replied, and I could tell he had a grin on his face. He loved to write things off. "He's the title sponsor of a little tournament near Cincinnati in a couple of weeks and he's filling some last-minute teams with people involved with

Charlotte. Wants the two of us paired with some money guys from up that way. Says we don't have to win."

"He must have seen you play before."

"Very funny. Just for that, you get to fly commercial."

"But you said you were sending the plane."

"That didn't work out. Emailing the details right now. Make it happen, and brush up on your New Testament."

"I already know more than most."

"You're right. In that case," he concluded, "try not to fuck this up."

2:00 P.M.

By the time I made it back to the office, the black beans were talking to me, and anybody else who would listen. This group would not have included Mildred. She was on the phone and hardly even noticed as I passed her desk on the way down the hall toward the first floor restrooms. The mechanical stack, the core of the building where the bathrooms and air conditioning systems are usually stacked on top of each other to maximize leasable square footage, was the only section of the interior not skinned in glass for obvious reasons. It seemed odd in the opening weeks of this building's life that everyone in the whole building could watch me walk toward the plumbing stack, and I was self-conscious in those early days. This was not one of those early days, and I would've threatened bodily harm to anyone standing between me and stall number two.

In the design process for a commercially viable office building, the emphasis is and must be on maximizing the return of every square foot, expending as little as possible to reap as much rent as possible. This equation leaves little room for embellishment. As one of the investors in my building, though, I took a little creative license with the restrooms, using only high-end fixtures and contemporary plumbing designs. Even on this day, once I settled into the business at hand, I relished the experience that I knew would justify what had occupied the bulk of my design time on the building. The floors, for example, were marble tiles that had been ordered for Elton John's, well, john. He'd decided, when they arrived, that the color wasn't quite right for his Buckhead penthouse potty, and the dealer had given me a great deal. Probably unremarkable tile, but great story. Consider, also, the carpentry that displaced the standard metal stall dividers, resulting in tight tolerances and supreme privacy, with only eight-inch gaps at the top and bottom of the door for ventilation.

I was admiring the interior finishes of stall two when the restroom door opened and leather heels marched softly across the floor. I didn't think much of it until the black leather shoes appeared in the lower eight of my stall door.

"Occupado," I said with sincerity and only the slightest hint of stating the obvious.

The black shoes then turned and backed their heels up to the lower eight of my stall door, a curious move that immediately got my attention. Then the stall door next to mine opened and a second set of leather soles made their way across Elton's marble and entered stall one. A tribute to the craftsmanship, I could hardly discern any sounds coming from the neighbor, save those that were quietly coming from the lower eight of their door. Still, the heels in my lower eight didn't move. And then the mumbling started. At first I thought it might just be noises that often accompany the digestive process, but it soon occurred to me that these mumblings lacked the enthusiasm or urgency usually associated with digestive utterances. Not that I'm an expert. And the mumbling seemed to be repetitive, like the person was saying the same thing over and over again, like he was praying or practicing a speech he was to deliver before a huge crowd. Suddenly, though, the volume reached a fevered pitch and sought me out with clarity.

"Are you listening to me, pretty boy?"

"What?" I replied, beginning to assume that the voice was talking to me. "Say again? I can hardly hear you." Again, such a testament to the restroom carpentry.

At this point the heels moved quickly from the lower eight while at the same time the door to stall one opened and a different pair of black leather toes appeared in the lower eight. Then it was just one shoe. Then the other shoe kicked in the door to stall two, and I was faced once again with a pair of large, angry men with buzz cuts and sunglasses. While this would have been a more timely occasion for a lesser man to shit his pants, the fact that my pants remained around my ankles paralyzed my fight or flight instincts. I did, however, muster the presence of mind to cover my loins, to the extent possible, with my cellphone.

"Have you been talking to me?" I asked?

"Shut the fuck up and let me do the talking," he said, leaning on the door post of stall two. "I think you know why I'm here, why we need to get to know one another in a spiritual sense. For the Bible teaches that we should all be looking out for our brothers. And you, my little friend, have got a brother who could damn well use some looking after."

"I have no idea what --" I offered, cut short by the man's arm reaching across the doorframe and slamming the door once again into the wall.

"You are your brother's keeper, and your brother is not behaving as a righteous man should. Your job is to bring your lost sheep back into the fold, back onto the path of righteousness. And if you're not up to it, we'll see if your lady friend is. All debts must be satisfied, all debtors forgiven."

With that, he turned and walked back across Elton's marble, followed closely by his associate. Neither looked back.

By the time I got my pants up and my feet beneath me, Mildred was knocking on the restroom door. This day was really shaping up.

"Hello," she asked with hesitance, "is there a problem?"

"No, Mildred," I mustered with my confident voice, meeting her at the door as I made my way out, "no problems here, other than the door to stall two will require some attention."

"Were those men friends of yours?"

"Did it sound like we were friendly?" I thought better about the tone of the reply after it was out, and offered a second try. "No, those men were not friends of mine, and I'm not entirely sure what they were after, but I am thankful that they have moved on."

"The one in the sunglasses was on drugs," she said, looking past me into the scene of the crime.

"Thank you, Mildred. Would you look in the file and determine which of the finish contractors worked on the bathrooms and see if they will come by and repair the door?"

"Okay. If they ask --"

"Tell them whatever you'd like, but don't mention the sunglasses and drugs theory. Just have them fix the door. And the wall."

Twenty minutes later I was sitting across from Thib in a window booth at the Waffle House around the corner from his residential storage unit. He, too, had been displaced by the keypad maintenance, though the need for it didn't seem to surprise him as much as I thought it should've.

"Are you stealing shit from the other units?" I asked with more than a hint of fraternal frustration, "cause I'm running dry on sympathy."

"Why do you assume it's me?"

"Thib, what other conclusions should I be drawing from all these connected points of light?"

"Not that I'm a thief, that's for sure. I should at least get the benefit of the doubt until proven guilty."

"You don't play the innocence card very convincingly, and the victim card is wearing pretty thin as well. You need some new material, and definitely a new audience."

The waitress brought the two sweet teas in large styrofoam cups and prepared to take our food orders. By now it was almost three in the afternoon, and I couldn't imagine anyone ordering food so far removed from standard meal times.

"Nothing for me, thanks."

"Patty Melt," Thib told the waitress, "scattered, smothered, covered and topped."

All I could do was stare at him, trying desperately to figure out how we could've emerged from the same biological parents.

"Look," he said, after putting the laminated menu back behind the napkin dispenser, "I didn't steal anything from the other units, but...."

"But what? But you know who did? But you were trying to sleep when they were cutting the ceiling wire three units over? But what?"

"Chad, dude, chill out. You're starting to hyperventilate. You're going to scare the staff into breaking out the defibrillator and lubing up the paddles."

I looked around to determine the sense of urgency felt by the staff. The cook was cleaning the grill and the lone waitress had called our order from the square on the far side of the grill and retreated to the stock room to continue her shift-change checklist. We were the only patrons. The staff was accustomed to much higher drama than we were offering.

"But what, Thib?"

"But I know who did."

"What a shock. Did you alert your landlord?"

"He knows all about it."

"What?"

"He knows all about it," Thib repeated calmly. "Pretty standard practice, apparently."

"Stealing from your tenants? How can that be standard practice?"

"Most of the shit's insured," Thib said calmly, "and sometimes the people actually pay to have it stolen. To collect without having to sell. Like those reality shows where they auction off the contents of a storage unit when the people have stopped paying the rent."

"So the people who rent the unit collect on their insurance?"

"Some of the time. Except for the pharmaceutical reps, apparently. The ones who keep samples in climate-controlled units."

"No insurance on those?"

"More complicated than that."

The waitress made fast work of delivering the patty melt and hash browns, placing the napkin and silverware alongside the plate and pulling a semi-full ketchup bottle from the next table before checking if we needed anything else and retreating to the checklist. So there was hardly a pause in Thib's story, though the story slowed as he began to eat.

"The drug reps never really report the thefts," he continued, "and I don't think there's insurance on that anyway."

"How do you know that?"

"I overheard a couple of the reps talking while they were moving product in or out of a unit down the hall. I think one was training the other because there were a lot of questions." He choked down a big bite of patty melt. "The one who seemed to be doing the training said that her unit had been broken into once, at another facility down by the airport, when she was working a different territory. But the company's unspoken perspective had been that product was making its way into the marketplace, and the samples had already been written off to marketing expense, so adding insurance adjusters to the mix hardly seemed efficient." He took another big bite of patty melt and squirted ketchup on the mound of hash browns.

"Are these controlled substances we're talking about?" I asked. "Like prescription drugs?"

"Pain meds mostly, I think, but I got nothing to do with all that. I just know the folks who did the recon work around the corner."

"Same people that seem to regard you as something of a lost sheep?"

"What?"

"The guys who were following me came back to visit me at the office. Said you were a lost sheep and I needed to get you back on the path to righteousness."

"Were they serious? I mean, who really says shit like that?"

"Serious enough to kick in the stall door and threaten Molly."

"She was in the bathroom?"

"No. I was. They threatened her if you didn't straighten up and fly right, follow the path of the righteous. Strange to hear those words spoken with an ominous tone from behind dark glasses."

"Probably Jeremiah's bulldogs. They seem to talk a lot about righteousness and brotherhood." He turned his attention back to the patty melt without giving me the satisfaction of being right. He used the corner of half of his sandwich to corral some wayward hash browns, dragging both through the ketchup.

"The guy from last night? I knew it."

"They all belong to this crazy church or cult. That's probably where the Biblical references come from, the righteousness and lost sheep. I think Jeremiah is some sort of Deacon or Bishop. They almost worship the guy. Crazy as hell."

"How did you get mixed up with these guys?"

"I did some work for one of the members of their little church. The guy owns a wholesale business for motorcycle parts. I built him a website with eCommerce capability and you'd think I had perfected cold fusion. That's how I met Jeremiah. They were interested in using technology to grow their congregation. So I started handling some IT projects for them."

I took a long pull from the styrofoam cup of tea and watched as Thib finished up the last of his food. Looking around the empty diner, it occurred to me how rapidly a person's life circumstances could change, for the better or worse. A twenty-dollar tip for our waitress, while not life-altering, might make an otherwise slow day worthwhile. Likewise, the last 48 hours had shown me just how quickly a life can be changed through events that are almost wholly unforeseeable. I guess I had always harbored a suspicion that my brother's road was substantially less travelled and considerably more dangerous. Otherwise, it might have come as a complete shock that he was actually living in the storage unit I rented to store his things "temporarily" while he and his girl at the time were working through some issues. But it was far from a shock, and according to the benchmarks of my chosen life, Thib was a lost sheep. But his life was his life, and he rarely seemed bothered by the inconvenience of his dependency on the kindness of the strange, the weird, and the unorthodox. And occasionally me. Still his life to lead.

"Please tell me that this Jeremiah guy isn't having me tailed because of a website. While I don't really want to know, this is all shaping up to reveal that you are in deeper than that."

"Not by choice or at least not by design."

"Imagine that."

August 15

"Let me get this straight. You want to create a desert so that tourists can experience the struggles of Moses as well as the temptations of Christ. But you want to create this experience alongside Pharoah's pursuit of the Jews and the parting of the Red Sea?"

"Exactly," Dan Richards replied with a generous note of enthusiasm for his own idea. "The way I envision it, folks will actually leave the desert experience through the parted Red Sea, maybe through a tank, like the ones they have at aquariums, where all the water flushes out and they walk through," he continued.

I was taking notes but couldn't harness the energy necessary to applaud or criticize the idea. I was just letting it flow over me. A couple of days had passed and the door to stall two was in good repair, but as much as I wanted to believe that the dust had settled, I realized that packaging a desert and a parting sea into a single experience was really the least of my concerns.

"That's an interesting concept."

"Yeah, I thought you'd like that," he said, and I can only imagine with a big grin. "But I'm not trying to do your job. You're the man when it comes to this creative stuff. I just thought I'd pass it along."

"Well I appreciate that. I'll just tweak your idea a little bit and then take full credit for it. Hope you don't mind."

"Wouldn't expect anything less. What kind of timeframe we looking at before you provide us with a glimpse of the poetry you hope to set in motion?"

"Well, I guess that all depends on how quickly you call me back with more of these ideas," I said with a sarcastic edge that would've gotten another man fired, in hopes, deep down, that it would get me fired. Dan Richards turned the other cheek.

"Don't look at me. I'm only part-time help. But we got shovels ready to start turning dirt, so we need to ramp this up a bit. Can you have a conceptual layout by the end of next week, you think?"

"I think that's doable," I replied, lying but comfortable with it. "But don't hold me to the site plan. Once I figure out how the Lord will work the place mysteriously, we can maximize the flow by moving some of the critical masses around. I'm just glad you didn't ask me to create the whole thing in six days."

"No, that's been done already. You're good, I hear, but you're not that good."

I hung up the phone with a chuckle and returned my attention to my notes, including the list of Bible stories that Mildred had provided. I wanted to get a broad brush layout on paper before I went back into the text to fish out details that would be meaningful, so I began placing potential "experiences" in a cluster to establish thematic relationships between them. Mangers next to mountain landscapes, crucifixes next to Canaan weddings. Rods to serpents and loaves to fishes. I had already begun to imagine the Tower of Babel as a drop ride, the kind that raises a bench full of people slowly and then releases them to simulate a free fall, only to engage the hydraulics at the last moment to soften the landing. I imagined the chaos of the tower to be accentuated by almost total darkness and the loud babbling of multiple voices speaking in various tongues. With some screams mixed in for good measure. It occurred to me now that a second side of that high point might also be used for viewing, like a

Mount Nebo or Pisgah, from which Moses was shown the Promised Land but denied entry into it. Maybe we should combine the many conversations between God and Moses, throw in some Commandments, and perhaps even a simulated burning bush. Great place for a snack bar.

I was trying to decide how best to divide the Old from the New Testament when my cellphone started moving across the top of my desk like a wide receiver from one of the old electric football games, vibrating toward the edge of the playing field. I picked it up but didn't recognize the number.

"Chad Felder," I said in a business casual sort of way.

"They say Lot was a righteous man," the voice said plainly, "despite the fact that he offered up his virgin daughters to the mob to spare the strangers." The voice didn't sound like Dan Richards, and I couldn't place it, though it seemed like a normal call in the context of mapping out a Biblical experience.

"Okay," I replied, looking down at the sketch. "Are you suggesting a Sodom and Gomorrah experience, because I don't know how that's going to play with the extreme fundamentalists."

"I don't know what the fuck you're talking about," the voice calmly replied, "but I had also assumed you to be a righteous man, a shepherd."

The hair on the back of my neck identified the caller, but the instinct was decidedly not flight. This game of charades had to stop. I had a divine experience to design and I had no interest in repairing any more bathrooms. I decided to hold a firm course.

"Listen, Jeremiah, I don't know what—"

"No, Tom Brokaw, you listen—"

"Chad?" It was Molly's voice, and it lifted me out of my chair and to the window to look toward the dumpster. No car.

"Molly?"

"They're looking for Thib," she said with frustration. "I've tried to find him, but he's not answering his phone."

"Where are you? Are you alright?"

"She's fine for now," Jeremiah said, returning to the phone, "and I do mean fine. And right now she is with me, and she plans to stay with me until your lost sheep is returned to the fold. As I prophesied two days ago, so shall it be, and the righteous man would know better than to call the law, for I am the law. As our Lord and Savior said in the Gospel of John, 'I am the way, the truth, and the life.' And that truth will set your woman free when it walks back in the door to be forgiven. And it's your job to find the truth, wherever it is hiding, and return it to me."

"You can't do this."

"Who are you to tell me what I can and cannot do, rich white boy? I don't get my authority from you. I am a soldier of the Lord, and this is His will I'm doing. So don't you ever get up in my face like that again. You do as you're told and we'll all be going to the mountaintop to sing some kumbayah. Now get to work, cause we'll be watching."

"Put Molly back on," I insisted, but he had already hung up. I hit the redial button on my phone.

"The number you have dialed has been disconnected or is no longer in service. Please check the number and dial again."

I hit the speed dial button reserved for Thib and got his voicemail.

"Listen, you little shit. I don't know what you've done to these guys, but they have kidnapped Molly. Call me NOW!"

I grabbed the jacket off the back of the door on my way out, just as the phone on my desk began to ring. I leapt back to the desk to check the caller ID. Bryan Thompson. His call would have to wait. I took the stairs two at a time and almost flew past Mildred's desk.

"Dan Richards on three," she said as I passed.

"Message." I was almost out the door as she continued.

"And somebody calling himself the jackal left you a message while you were on the phone with Mr. Richards earlier." The sound of the name stopped me like a concrete wall. I turned back toward Mildred.

"Are you sure he didn't say Jack or Jacko? Anything like that?"

"Quite sure. He repeated it when I asked him to."

"Didn't that seem odd to you?"

"Well," she replied over the top of her reading glasses, "at least he wasn't kicking the doors in. Given your history lately, nothing seems odd these days." She held the pink slip up to my reach while turning her gaze back to the tidy landscape of her desk. "Said to call him at that number."

I looked down at the number as I turned and walked out the door to the parking lot and my car. I glanced once again to check the spaces around the dumpster. No dark Lexus with tinted windows. No cars at all, in fact. I got in my car and called the number on the pink slip. A familiar voice answered.

"Sorry about all the covert stuff, bro. Things have heated up in the last couple of days."

"Don't give me that bro shit, Thib. They've got Molly."

"No shit?"

"No shit. I just got off the phone with your buddy Jeremiah. Now where are we meeting, and I mean right now. I've had enough of your fun, and I don't get my wife back until I herd you back into their barnyard."

"It's not that easy."

"You're damn right it's that easy. Where are you?"

"That doesn't matter. It's gotten more complicated."

"Nothing complicated about swapping you back to them for my wife, and I don't want to know any more about all of this. I don't care what you've done or what they've done. I just want my wife and my life back."

"Market rate a little higher on the second wife than the blood brother?"

"Don't pull that crap on me. Just tell me where you are and let me come to you."

"They'll have somebody on you."

"I'm sitting in the parking lot and there is no Lexus to be found."

"Don't be stupid. They know where you are."

There passed an awkward silence as I considered the likelihood that Thib was right about my being followed, and probably about the market rate for blood brothers as well.

"He said for me not to call the cops," I said with building frustration, "so what do you want me to do? You're the one that made the enemies, and now you want Molly to pay the price? What the fuck, Thib?"

"He won't hurt Molly, or anybody else for that matter."

"How do you know? You keep saying what he won't do, but he keeps on doing things. Listen to me, Thib. You've got to make this right, man. Where are you? I'm coming to get you right now so we can get this worked out."

There was another silence. I started the car in hopes that the activity might strengthen my argument and the noise would drive the point home. It apparently worked.

"You know the Stonehenge development, out on 29 past the Walgreen's?"

"Yeah, why?"

"Come to the back of that development, a short-block street, Druid Lane. Turn the car around and park facing out and kill the headlights. Keep the car running, though, and keep your phone on."

I was halfway out of the parking lot by the time we ended the call. Thib hadn't needed to, but he reminded me to be careful about being followed. I watched the mirrors like a hawk as I made my way back into the commercial districts that seemed to appear overnight, strip malls along high-traffic corridors connecting glass office buildings with residential developments, both labeled with equal pretense. Crescent Commerce and Watermark Capital Centre reflected the sun's warmth onto home centers and wholesale club warehouses and sports equipment franchises, and the big box retailers cast a shadow on the residential likes of Watership Down and Indian Hills and, somewhere behind a chain pharmacy, Stonehenge.

I hadn't been on the road long before I noticed what I thought was a car tailing me. Sunset had given way to dusk, and headlights made it more difficult to differentiate between cars, but I could recognize the distinctive headlights of an early '90s Buick Century from a mile away, and a pair of those headlights moved in and out of traffic with me with increasing predictability. How does a kidnapping thug go from a tinted, late-model Lexus to a relic from the early Clinton Administration? But there it was, doing a really bad job of following me. And these idiots had kidnapped my wife?

I was still ten or fifteen minutes from the Stonehenge development, but I needed to lose the Buick before I got too close. I pointed my car toward a brightly lit home improvement warehouse and cut quickly across two lanes of disgruntled traffic to make the entrance to the strip mall just in time. Without looking back I pulled through the parking lot and turned my car around to face the same entrance I'd just come through. Sure enough, the Buick made the turn into the lot and then slowly eased into a spot far across the lot, facing me, beneath a light in such a way that I couldn't see in the car. Then the headlights went dark. I still couldn't make out any passengers, and nobody got out of the car. After a couple of minutes I decided to force their hand.

As I eased across the parking lot and the reflection from the light above diminished, I was able to see into the car. But there was nobody in it. The closer I got to the car, the more apparent it became that no heads or bodies appeared in the windshield. I circled wide, maybe fifty yards from the car, to get a look from the side and then from the rear, but the tinted windows, if they were even tinted, clearly showed a steering wheel and dashboard and small, rectangular headrests on the front bench seat. I could not have imagined this car's recent move to this spot, and it seemed unlikely that I would have missed the driver's hasty exit from the car if I was watching it from directly in front, regardless of the distance. Hell, even if he'd climbed out a window I would've noticed. So the driver was still in the car. And this was because he knew I'd spotted the tail and was unwilling to show himself. Emboldened by this thought, I circled more closely a second time and a third until pulling directly alongside the Buick, driver's window to driver's window, door to door. I rolled the window down but left the engine running and the transmission in gear. If the guy pulled a gun this time I was taking no chances.

"Hello?" I called out to the Buick's window. No response. "Anybody in there?"

Resigned to the utter mystery of it all, and in a hurry, I was ready to admit my own paranoia. But first, I needed to take a look, just to be sure. I put the car in gear and opened my door, got out and took a couple of steps to close the short distance between the cars. As I cupped my hands around my eyes to block out the glare from the light above and leaned toward the Buick's window, a flash of bright metal clanged against the window. I jumped a step back and reached for my own car door but stopped when I realized the flash of metal was a badge that then disappeared from the window as the Buick's door opened and two Converse sneakers appeared, touched ground, and gave way to a face I recognized but couldn't name. She stepped out of the car and shoved the badge back into her pocket, the one right behind the gun on her right hip.

"Aren't you Thib's girlfriend?" I said to the woman, wanting to scratch my head but not really wanting to make any sudden moves. "Carol? Something like that?"

"Calliope, yes," she replied, almost blushing with embarrassment, but that's not my real name."

"That must have something to do with the badge and the gun," I said, looking at my watch, "and the fact that you're following me. Just clear up that last part, if you would, and I'll be on my way."

"You going to meet with him?"

"Who is him?"

"Your brother," she replied without rolling her eyes or making any of the noises or gestures I would have expected from an estranged and disgruntled girlfriend who, unable to find her man, had settled on following his more stable brother back to him.

"I have no idea what you're talking about."

"I think you do."

"So who are you and why are you following me?"

"Agent Wagner," she said, bringing the badge back out for formal review, "Georgia Bureau of Investigation. I'm not at liberty to discuss the details of the investigation, but I think you know by now that your brother is involved."

"So you're not a bartender sleeping with my brother in a storage unit?" Her facial expression changed only slightly and she didn't look away or avoid the question. She didn't answer it, either.

"Your brother is involved with a network of individuals, some of whom you've met, who are the focus of our investigation. Thib has fallen silent over the last several days and I'm simply trying to reconnect."

"And you're following me because you think I know where he is?"

"I was until you jumped across three lanes of traffic."

"Well, I hate to disappoint you, but I haven't talked to him in days myself. He usually calls me when he needs money."

"So, where you heading?"

"Meeting my wife for dinner, and running late as usual, so if you'll excuse me."

"And sensitive to being followed on the way to dinner with your wife? That doesn't make sense."

"Paranoid, I guess," I replied, putting one hand on the car door and turning back to face Agent Wagner. "Like you said, I've met some of the folks you're investigating." I had one foot in the car when her reply stopped me cold.

"The same ones that have your wife?"

"How do you know about that?"

"Look," she said, closing her car door and walking toward me, "I may not be able to tail a car worth a shit in fog and traffic, but I'm actually pretty good at the other parts of my job. Is he expecting you alone and in this car?"

"Yes."

"Then how about I tag along and fill you in on the way?" She hadn't really expected an answer when she made the statement, and she'd slid into the back seat before I could assemble a response. I started the car and pulled back into traffic to make my way to Stonehenge, my unexpected passenger settling herself deep into the back seat, presumably because being discovered twice in one night was against policy.

"Fire when ready, whatever your name is, cause none of this shit makes sense to me. You seem to have all the answers, so don't bother waiting for the questions."

"Wagner. Louisa Wagner. And I don't have all the answers. Couldn't share them even if I did."

"But," I said interrupting her, "the fact that you're hiding in the back seat of my car can't be good."

"Some parts of this have been in process for longer than I've been with the Bureau."

"And how long has that been?" I said, trying to hide my assumption that she was very new to her job.

"About three years. Atlanta Police before that. But this particular group has been on the radar for a while."

"Including my brother?"

"Nope. New face as of about a year ago. We don't really know how deep his roots go into the bad soil, so to say, but he must know more than we thought if Jeremiah is working this hard to rein him in."

"And this is all about the missing stuff from the storage units?"

"I don't know anything about that," she said with a chuckle," but I've gotten to know Thib well enough to know that his curiosity runs a bit wilder than that."

"Like sex in a storage unit?" I pulled to a stop at a red light and looked back in the mirror to make eye contact deep in the back seat. Her eyes didn't meet mine, but looked out the window for landmarks.

"Please tell me you're not casting the first stone. It's a little late for that, don't you think?"

I had to smile at her presumption. She didn't know a damn thing about me. Or did she? What could she know? What could Thib have told her while they were shacked up among the tombstones of American consumerism?

"Where are you meeting him?" she asked, trying to connect the seemingly endless strip malls with an ultimate destination.

"Stonehenge. Residential. Behind the Walgreen's up ahead."

"I'm familiar. We worked a couple of cases in that neighborhood last year."

"What sort of cases?"

"Preliminary stuff for DEA, I think."

"Drugs. That figures." The light had turned green and was getting the car back up to speed when the Walgreen's came into sight well down the road.

"From what I remember, there are parts of that development that never quite filled out," she said, "where the houses were built, or mostly built, but never occupied."

"I think the original ownership structure went bust. At least that's what I heard. They had a conservator in place for the wetlands area they built around, but I don't know what happened to the community assets and the owner's association. I assume one of the banks absorbed it."

"We busted a small lab on the back side of the lake. Kids mostly, but there was almost a residential quality to the cluster of foreclosed houses, like they were abandoned but anything but vacant."

We turned off the main road at the Walgreen's and drove less than a half mile before reaching the entrance to Stonehenge, an inviting and well-lit mixture of large stones and split-rail fencing with the requisite but empty guard hut. Easing through the gates and onto the main street, I noticed that the houses seemed vibrant and relevant, like families lived there and paid the power bill and mowed the yard on Saturdays and yelled at the cable news pundits like regular people. About two blocks in, though, the scene began to shift. Though the streetlights remained on, every third house now seemed empty and dark, the yard unattended, the pundits silenced. The next block shifted the malaise to every other house, and a view across a small lake—a pond, really—substantiated the assumption that the scene was the same from the back yards. Despite the sign at the front warning of 24-hour surveillance, not a creature was stirring. The only badge in the place was tucked down in my back seat as I made my way around to the back side of the lake in search of Druid Lane.

By the time I reached Druid Lane all the houses were dark, the driveways empty, the yards unattended. In some cases it seemed as if the turf and plant matter had been repossessed or appropriated by a neighbor. All of the houses seemed to back up to a wooded area, as if the street had been carved out of the forest, and the streetscape was missing the full complement of street lights. The two on the corners entering the street were working, but the deeper I drove toward the eventual cul-de-sac, the more noticeable the absence of light became. The poles and fixtures were still intact, but the bulbs offered nothing. As instructed, I turned the car around and pointed my line of sight back toward the working streetlights and the lake and the gate and Walgreen's beyond, killed the headlights, idled the engine, and waited.

"What are you waiting for?" came the voice from the back seat.

"Just doing what I was told to do."

We sat quietly in the darkness. Nothing moved. There were no other headlights. No porch or garage lights responded to motion detectors. Even the dash lights seemed bright, so I found the dimmer switch to the left of the steering wheel and dimmed them. The absolute quiet revealed a small melody, and I reached down to turn the radio off. I fumbled with the buttons on my door's armrest until I found the right one and ensured the doors were unlocked.

"They unlock automatically when you put the car in park," came the voice from the back seat.

I closed my eyes and let my head fall back against the headrest, reminded of my wife's knack for stating the obvious. Suddenly, the passenger door clicked and lurched open. Thib fell into the seat with a sigh as our eyes met, both sets temporarily blinded by the dome light on the ceiling between us. He reached and pulled his door closed, extinguishing the light in the process, and turned back to face me.

"Doesn't look like you were followed."

"I wouldn't go that far," I said, putting the car in drive and automatically locking the doors and moving down the street before my passengers had the chance to get reacquainted.

"What does that mean?"

"He means," came the voice from the back seat, "that it's a little more complicated than that."

"Calliope?" Thib asked, jerking his head around the headrest.

"Not exactly," I said, rounding the corner between the two working streetlights and making my way around the lake toward the gates.

8:00 P.M.

Holy Guardian Church was a small, unassuming red brick structure that, in a previous iteration, had been a simple country church of the Apostolic or Pentecostal variety. I had passed the building a million times on the way to the interstate, but it had never really caught my eye. From its hillside perch overlooking I-85, Holy Guardian bore witness to an admittedly declining commercial corridor. The path of progress had bypassed the little congregation in the 1970s, and the bloom was almost completely off the rose by the end of Y2K. Fortunately, a young minister was looking to plant an ecumenical seed and minister to the growing population in Suburban Northeast Atlanta, and so it came to pass that Reverend Elijah Oates struck a deal with the few remaining congregants and Holy Guardian was born. The most interesting detail of the transaction, according to Agent Wagner, was that no mortgage was ever recorded. Reverend Elijah Oates had paid cash for his church start-up, and one could only assume that the seed money had come from his brother, Bishop Jeremiah Oates, the lunatic who currently had my wife but wanted my brother.

"I can't believe I got played by the GBI," Thib groaned as he watched the traffic flow past his window, "though you have to admit that's pretty fucking cool." He looked in my direction and said this despite the fact that Agent Wagner was still with us, talking quietly on her phone in the back seat. I swear the man lives in a parallel universe.

"At this point I don't think it becomes a badge of honor," I replied, though he had already swiveled his grin back to the traffic as we wove our way through

Sherman toward the interstate, both of us trying to assimilate the information provided by Agent Wagner.

"Okay," she said, having ended the phone conversation, "there will be a strip mall ahead with an Office Depot, on the right. Pull in there and drop me in front of the store. And here's how this all plays out. I was never here, and as far as the world knows, I'm still Calliope."

"That's going to be pretty tough."

"Shut up, Thib," I snapped. "Let the nice agent tell us how we're going to clean up your mess." I'd like to say I instantly regretted the breach of brotherly love, but his interests were no longer my concerns. Shithead.

"And here's the tricky part," she continued, "this is not to be approached as a kidnapping or a hostage situation."

"What?"

"You have to downplay the whole thing."

"That doesn't even make sense," I protested, wanting to settle this issue as the Office Depot began to emerge on the horizon. "I thought you were on the phone calling in the cavalry just now. I was expecting a little, you know, support, some tax dollars rolling in with lights flashing and guns blazing. These assholes kidnapped my wife, for God's sake! And now you want me to go in and shake hands and apologize for the delay?"

"Well, not that exactly," she said, eyeing the landscape and readying to remove herself from the car, "but I think you get the point. If you want these guys to pay for their sins, you can't stop the game just yet. If you do that, if you raise any flags, all the work we've done over the last several years goes down the toilet. And if you do that right now, we can't be there to control the situation. You want us to be able to control the situation."

"Seems like a gun and a badge would offer some element of control," I offered, slowing to make the turn into the parking lot. "If not control, at least some piece of mind. I get the feeling we're bringing a banana to a knife fight." This drew an unintended chuckle from Thib. I silenced it with a sideways glance.

"These guys are not characteristically violent," Wagner said.

"You didn't see the stall door at my office."

"If they were violent, we wouldn't be having this conversation," she said, turning to look out the back window of the car. "And your brother would've been dead a couple of months ago."

I had no more details than that as, a couple of minutes later, I pulled into the parking lot of Holy Guardian Church, shepherding a lost sheep like a righteous man should. I didn't want to, but I was prepared to trade brother for wife. There were only a couple of cars parked in the section of lot around the back side of the hill, a well-lit area also bordered by hardwood trees and the lights of the interstate beyond. As directed, we parked the car near the rear entrance, a set of doors one floor below what was obviously the sanctuary or community space of the church. A single exposed bulb hung from the ceiling above the white painted doors. I pulled on both handles but neither door opened. I knocked on the door and heard what sounded like an aluminum folding chair slide across the floor from inside. Seconds later, the door opened slightly, a familiar set of eyes met mine, and the door opened wider to allow us to step into the room.

As my eyes adjusted to the stark whiteness of the fluorescent ceiling fixtures, I scanned the room until I found Molly, first standing from the chair where she'd been sitting and then walking quickly toward me dressed in yoga pants and a sports bra.

"What have they done?" I said, wrapping my arms around her and making every effort to cover her exposed skin. "Are you all right?"

"I'm fine," she replied into the hug. "Just cold. It's freezing down here."

"What happened to your clothes?" I feared the worst.

"I had just finished a workout. My jacket is in my car, back at the club."

I turned and faced her captors, though I couldn't call them that, and realized that neither of them was Jeremiah.

"Well," I said in the direction of the two men and with a nod in Thib's direction, "looks like everybody got what they came for, so I believe we'll leave you to work out the details. Just tell Jeremiah that the righteous man has delivered the sheep."

My attempt at nonchalance got a rise out of Molly who was, nonetheless, anxious to leave the room. As we turned and made our way toward the door, however, one of the well-dressed types eased to his right, indicating his intention to block the door if we insisted on leaving so soon.

"This doesn't even make sense," I said in a loud and frustrated voice. "We have nothing to do with whatever you're doing, don't know anything about it, and don't want to know anything about it. Your business is your business, and it ought to stay that way as far as I'm concerned."

"Well, that's all fine and good, Tom Brokaw, but the Lord works in mysterious ways, his wonders to reveal." Jeremiah seemed to be speaking while descending a staircase I couldn't see. His voice was getting incrementally clearer. "And I don't think he gives a shit if it makes sense to you," he continued, rounding a corner into view. "I know I don't."

Jeremiah Oates—it was somehow comforting to know his last name—strode across the small room with confidence and ease, allowing his eyes to linger on my wife's form a little too long. He stopped in front of us and ran his left hand along Molly's bare arm. "His wonders to reveal. Yes, ma'am." She never flinched. He then walked over to a small folding chair near the other men, sat, and slowly crossed his right leg over his left and locked his fingers behind his head, never taking his eyes from our direction.

"What I can't figure," he said, to nobody in particular, allowing his head to rest in his hands, baring his throat like a wolf when he knows no threat, "is how a fine woman like that ends up with either one of you. One of you knows things he ain't telling, and the other don't know a damn thing and won't shut up." There was a pause that would have begged an answer had a question been posed. "Well, Tom Brokaw? You mighty quiet over there. Ain't you got even the least bit of curiosity about all this? Cause you in it now, like it or not."

"Nope. I don't want to know. My brother is an adult and, as an adult, makes his own way. Your business with him has nothing to do with me or my family."

"So a man shall leave his parents and cleave to his wife, and the two shall become one flesh."

"If you say so."

"Come on now, Tom Brokaw. The prodigal here tells me you preached the gospel back in the day. We are brothers, you and I, men of God, bathed in the blood, wrapped in the blessed warmth of the Word. Share some verse with a brother."

"That was a long time ago."

"No good news? No message of hope?"

"Just want to go home."

"Then let's hope that my brother from another mother, Sweet Boudreaux, has some good news for all of us, cause nobody's going home until the plate is passed and some singing is done. What you say over there, Boudreaux? You got a little something to put in the plate?"

Thib looked at me almost in apology. I had no idea what he'd gotten himself into, and he was ill-prepared to hang his dirty laundry out for me to see. I almost felt sorry for him. Were it not for the dozens of times I'd cleaned up his messes, he might have gotten a response from me. But I felt nothing.

"I've got what you asked for," Thib told Jeremiah, turning his eyes from me to Jeremiah as he continued, "but not in a form that you can use."

"How do you know what I can or cannot use," Jeremiah replied, unfolding his hands and standing, cracking his neck and smoothing the sleeves of his suit jacket. "Why don't you let me make those decisions."

"What I mean is that I have no way to transfer the product into your hands. It is safely stored and protected, but I don't have it on me."

"But you can access it?"

"From anywhere."

Jeremiah nodded and seemed to consider Thib's information before turning slightly to his left and signaling the thugs standing behind him at the card table. One of the men reached under the table and produced a black leather briefcase with an accordion top. He reached in slowly, and I imagined for an instant that he would withdraw a gun. Instead, he removed a laptop computer and cellphone tether, cleared the cards from the table, and assembled the combination of electronics on the table. Satisfied that all preparations were made, but without looking back to confirm, Jeremiah motioned to the table and even pulled a folding chair from under, offering Thib a seat.

"I anticipated that you might play that card," he said, "so I brought the game to you."

Thib made his way slowly to the table, took the offered seat, and began working on the laptop. Jeremiah stood over his shoulder looking intently at every keystroke. I was confused to say the least.

"So all of this is about some computer game?"

"This is not a game," Jeremiah said without looking up. He continued as if he were calling play-by-play. "The prodigal son here is killing the fatted calf, Tom Brokaw, and right before your eyes the Lord is shining his countenance upon us."

"What's that supposed to mean?"

"That means money, Tom Brokaw. That means that Boudreaux here, the brother you forsake for jumping the reservation and leaving you to uphold the family name and all that other shit that rich white folks seem to care about, is one very smart white boy. At this very moment, College Boy here is downloading the names, account numbers, and PINs of random debit card transactions processed by the three largest grocery chains in the metro area."

"Identity theft?"

"Not when you consider that these good people meant to tithe. These good folks had every intention of supporting the Lord's work in small, random increments through the next statement cycle. And the one beyond that if they don't notice. And most of them won't."

Thib said nothing while the data dump took place. He didn't look up and he didn't change his facial expression. I looked at Molly and she seemed only anxious to leave. Her capacity to judge was hostage to the utter simplicity of her life, I thought. The small transactions on the debit cards of strangers would not affect housing sales or the gym's operating hours. The alarming lack of concern made my own reaction seem exaggerated, and I was relieved when Thib stood up.

"Done," he said.

"Nice work, Boudreaux," Jeremiah replied, slapping him on the back. "Forgiveness is yours. Go forth and sin no more!"

Thib turned and walked toward the door. The goon at the gate stepped aside. Thib looked back as if to say the bar was out of liquor and it was time to go. I thought it strange how calmly the whole situation resolved itself.

"What happens now?" I asked Jeremiah.

"Phase Two," he replied calmly. "I got a tech-savvy brother sitting in a coffee shop across town that will slip this little jewel into play, and the rest will be forensic accounting, as they say. Some of that CSI: Wall Street shit.

"I meant with us."

"Y'all free at last, free at last," he replied without the slightest hint of sarcasm or irony. "And I hope our time together has given you some peace and quiet."

While my mind was neither peaceful nor quiet, the atmosphere in the car was easily both of those. Thib sat in the back seat and said nothing as we pulled away from the church and back into traffic. Molly sat with her arms folded across her chest, eyes closed and jaw tight. She didn't say a word all the way back to the gym. Once there, she got out, got in her car, and drove away. Thib remained in the back seat.

"I don't believe she's too happy," he said as we pulled away. I couldn't muster a response and dared not even look in the mirror. I pulled the car back into traffic and headed for the mini-storage. Neither of us spoke until I pulled the car into the parking lot and up to the door, without taking the car out of gear.

"Come on, Bro," he said, putting his hand on the door handle, "tomorrow's another day, right?"

"Just try to fuck up somebody else's life tomorrow, Bro," I replied without hesitation, exaggerating the urban slang. "Ain't no meat left on this bone."

He got out and had barely closed the door as I pulled away, circled the small lot, and exited the same way I'd come in, all without the slightest hint of eye contact.

The drive home was a blur. While I should have been running scenarios by which I would salvage my marriage, I chose instead to inventory my brother's history, searching for wrong turns, bad influences, any early signals that might help explain why he seemed to have a tendency to step in the really deep shit, unlike the rest of us who have our occasional bouts with the shallow but predictable piles.

Certainly our parents could be queued up as contributing factors. Our mother's suicide left us all in a lurch, so to say. As the youngest, Thib was potentially the most attached, but healthy people assisted by helpful therapists usually move through that emotional mine field. And Thib had seen his share of therapists. Our father had seen to that. Matching child with shrink and shrink with meds was part of what a pharmacist did in the early days of pharmacotherapy. I couldn't help but think that we'd one day look back at Ritalin and Aderall with similar wonder. I had developed dozens of sites for national drug store chains and every single one brought back memories of my father behind the elevated counter at the back of his pharmacy, glasses on the end of his nose or in the pocket of his white lab coat.

Then there was the portable shock treatment machine we experimented with at the kitchen table. Dialing for dopamine, I think he called it. Or maybe that's just a name I gave it now, remembering the little blue suitcase for the first time in decades. My mother had never liked it, even when her psychiatrist had recommended it as a companion therapy to the Valium. But Thib had almost reveled in the challenge of the thing, much like a strong-willed dog might battle mightily against a modern invisible fence mechanism, taking the pain until the transmitter's battery failed and his boundaries ceased to exist.

Thib had always been a big fan of testing boundaries. He had been the kind of kid who knew how to push buttons in a strange Pavlovian medley, quietly working people to his side despite everyone's recognition, all along, that his side was time and energy wasted. Though our father had never been a violent man, I remember now a handful of occasions when Thib yanked his chain to the point of abject frustration and the laying on of the hands in a less than spiritual fashion. Now in my 40s, childless and steaming toward the end of a second marriage, I began to empathize with my father, trying to balance the love I knew I should feel for my brother with the adult recognition of his own peculiar failure to launch. I knew I could never save him. The jury was still out on me.

Back at the house, I pulled into the driveway alongside an upturned trash can, punctuating the day beautifully. I backed the car back into the road to allow the headlights to brighten the task that lay ahead. The neighborhood dogs had made a real mess of our tidy refuse. I used a shoebox to scoop much of the debris back into the can. An interesting choice, I thought, since I hadn't liked the shoes she bought anyway. After 4 or 5 scoops, my eyes were drawn to a peculiar site at the bottom of the shoe box, under a large lettuce leaf. It was a small box about the size of a smart phone, and it had at one point contained a pregnancy test.

August 24

Jason Sharp was no ordinary developer. His early successes included mixed-use industrial and residential complexes, a combination that no one could ever have predicted as viable, and high-density residential development along retired military bases in small Midwestern towns that had all but dried up. Jason Sharp had pulled more than one rabbit out of his hat, and the world seemed to be a better place for it. The markets in which he had worked were all foreign to me, so I was not privy to the details or the opinions of the locals. The trade magazines, however, had branded Jason Sharp a rising star almost from the very beginning. He had studied architecture at Princeton, so was by no stretch of the imagination a Luddite within the design community. But Jason Sharp, who grown up lower middle class in lower middle Alabama, was drawn initially to the money side of the equation. And while his architecture skills were certainly an asset along the way, strip malls and metal buildings rarely required a gifted designer.

Shortly after our initial flyover, I met with Jason at the Atlanta airport. He was passing through town, connecting in Atlanta as everyone seemed to do, and wanted to spend his two-hour layover productively. I caught up with him in a bar in the main terminal as he was stirring what appeared to be his 3rd scotch.

"I don't know if you realize this from our time together in that really small airplane," he said after making initial eye contact, "but I am not a big fan of flying. I choose to self-medicate, and I do so liberally."

"It was a mighty small airplane," I said trying to establish a point of connection.

"Would you care to join me?"

"Well, I usually like to wait until the noon hour passes," I said with a smile and nod, "but I'm sure the blonde behind the bar over there will have something I can drink." When I returned from the bar, Jason had opened the folder on the small bar table and was using a mechanical pencil to make small notes. The top sheet in the folder appeared to be a site plan, a view of the theme park as he envisioned it completed.

"So Dan thinks you're the concept guy," he said without looking up. "The English major in the woodpile, it seems. I'm assuming you've been giving this your full attention, but you really ought to know that we need a compelling story pretty early in the process. The rest of us, though we can doodle ahead of time, are waiting on you."

"No pressure there."

"None intended. Heightened awareness. That's all."

"Well, I appreciate that. Your assumption is correct, and this is the primary project on my table right now. But since you've got your toys out and ready to play, why don't you give me your ideas on how you see this experience flowing from beginning to end."

"Standard Disney fare, if you ask me. The site plan I have developed takes no details into account. These blocks are just way stations between the entrance and exit. Each of the interactive spaces will need to be designed individually once we understand the larger mission or purpose of the experience."

"And you see each of these interactive spaces as emerging from some Biblical context," I asked, dipping a toe into the religion conversation.

"I think that's what Dan Richards has in mind," he replied, looking up long enough to stir his drink and lock eyes. "I try to take the client's ideas and deliver a product that exceeds all their expectations. So let's start with the assumption that each and every visitor to this site will, in some form or fashion, engage the Holy Spirit. I don't think it's a measure that Richards would hold us to, but it would be damn nice to hit it."

"Have you done projects like this before?"

"Of a religious nature? Is that what you mean?"

"More or less, yes."

"Or are you skipping ahead to the real question? Are you really asking if I'm aware of the fact that my client is asking me to develop a very expensive Jonestown, where the Kool-Aid won't kill you but the onion rings might?"

"Projects of a religious nature," I offered quickly, trying to dispel any hint that I thought the project's prospects were anything but promising. "I'm not making a judgment, about you or the project. Just trying to get the lay of the land."

"Dan Richards is a funny fellow," he said looking in my direction. "To the world he seems like a savvy businessman, and his success in the car business is a daily testament to those skills. But his real passion has nothing to do with the car business. Sometimes I think he's been trapped in that life because of marriage, lifestyle, or any of a million choices that each of us make that deliver us to the shores of where we are today."

The scotch seemed to be dulling Mr. Sharp, and I settled in for what I thought would be a long philosophical treatise as a young waitress delivered an ice cold Coke in a tall glass. Tall enough, I hoped, to get me through this conversation. I stirred the ice despite the absence of alcohol. Old habits die hard.

"His real passion is doing the Lord's work," he continued where he left off. "It's an important part of everything he does. But to answer your initial question, the only other project like this in my portfolio is a master plan for a church school in Northern Kentucky. I met Dan Richards through that project."

"Nice work if you can get it," I said after a long pause. "I'm just happy to be involved."

"What about you? Have you done a lot of religious projects?"

"This one's a first. This is a whole new concept for me, combining religious experience with capitalism, almost deifying the Mouse, if you will."

"But you have some history with these ideas," he asked, searching my face for some indication of shock or embarrassment. "Somebody said you actually had some seminary in your background, a real come to Jesus meeting."

"Long time ago in a place far, far away," I replied with a grin. "I guess if you look at it the right way, that was actually my first experience with the conflict between religious experience and capitalism. I couldn't reconcile the two to my satisfaction, so I deferred to the greater calling."

"How, then, do you suggest we reconcile them for the purposes of this project?"

"I guess that's the easy part of this exercise," I replied without thinking. "Our responsibility to this group and to Dan Richards is purely capitalistic. The stories I create and the spaces you design will be, for us, commercial spaces, requiring some anticipation of revenue per square foot like any other. At least that's the way I see it. The expectation is different for Dan Richards and for the millions of visitors he hopes to draw to this experience. It is, for them, a religious experience, and I hope to facilitate that experience to the very limits of my imagination and my capacity to empathize with other humans. To be perfectly honest, though, I don't anticipate any great revelations or moments of spiritual clarity as a result of this project."

"I believe we plow similar ground there," he said before raising his scotch and draining the glass. "One might argue that I have worshiped too long at the foot of the dollar to turn back now. But I was never a great believer to begin with. I guess I like the idea of belief, but run enough bad water under a bridge and before long the creek just looks dirty. So you were a preacher for a while?"

"Very briefly. As I said, the vow of austerity wasn't really my thing. And then came the doubt and the questions and the irreconcilable certainty. I guess that was the hardest part. Sometimes I think the ones with all the answers are the same ones that climb on the bus with a bomb strapped to their midsection. I couldn't visualize that strong sense of certainty in my future."

"You must've seen it at some point, further back, to have gone through all that schooling."

"Probably more that it just seemed like the right thing to do at the time. It might just as well have been business school or architecture school. For whatever reason it seemed like the clearest path for me."

"Well, lucky for us," he said, refocusing his attention on the papers on the bar table, "because we need to tap into that former life of yours to exceed the expectations of one Dan Richards. So does the story begin in the Garden of Eden?"

"I see that as a likely place to start, if the experience is going to include other stories from the Old Testament. Alternatively, we could focus on the New Testament and avoid many of the intellectual pitfalls of the older books."

"I don't think anybody sees this as an intellectual pursuit," he replied with a chuckle. "Even Dan Richards doesn't see this as an intellectual pursuit. I think we need to mix in all of the old stories that are both scary and exciting, even the violent ones, because that's what will make for an interesting and memorable experience. Otherwise, we're building a series of lecture halls where somebody's going to tell Sunday school stories to little boys and girls on their way to a gift shop."

"So are we talking about roller coasters?"

"Even log rides, if that's what it takes. Like the parting of the Red Sea at just the right moment. Whatever it takes to bring these old stories back to life in a way that will make them relevant to kids. Imagine creating a theatrical experience of the resurrection, complete with the blowing wind of the Holy Spirit and the tactile experience of the stone being rolled away from the door." At this point Jason Sharp began referring to his notes, searching the margins for the best ideas and using the drafting pencil to point to natural spots on the site plan. I sat back in my chair and listened as he walked me through Eden, a tropical paradise inhabited by Adam and Eve and the occasional dinosaur.

"But that doesn't even make sense," I objected when he mentioned the dinosaur. "Science tells us that humans and dinosaurs didn't exist at the same time."

"But your market, your target demographic, has no interest in what science tells us. The fundamentalist perspective, at least among Christians, is that the Bible is the inerrant word of God and the earth is 6,000 years old. These are the people we hope to attract, to entertain, and to send out into the world to recruit more visitors. Our opinions, yours and mine, may differ from that perspective, but our task here is to create that experience. That is the goal as Dan Richards defines it."

"So does he define himself as a fundamentalist? And does he value these same perspectives?"

"He does, though he will not hold you to them. My hunch is that he values our expertise in creating this experience as he envisions it. However, I wouldn't go wearing your true feelings on your sleeve, if you know what I mean."

"So, like the Garden of Eden, we should approach each of these stories, which ever ones we choose, as real events. So, Noah and the Ark captures an event in historically accurate terms. Is that correct?"

"Sure. Why not? From the way it is described, it was a really big boat. Don't overthink it."

So I was in the process of trying not to overthink it about a week later as we gathered around a conference table to consider the possibilities. All the players were there. Dan Richards was there, on his way from a dealer convention in Las Vegas to a major car show in Manhattan. His stopover in Charlotte, a spot chosen by Jason Sharp for its proximity to the site, would be brief but he was easily the most enthusiastic of the bunch. Flying into town over the patch of dirt he owned out by the airport would also boost Dan's enthusiasm, in case he was frustrated that the project was lagging behind. Sharp was also present, leading the discussion and playing host in a nondescript meeting room housed in a corner of one of the top floors of a building owned and primarily occupied by one of the top banks in the country. The top floors had been reserved for a private club, one that reciprocated with Sharp's own club back in whatever town he rarely visited. Bryan Thompson had made the short drive up from Greenville, South Carolina. His role in the venture was a bit more cut and dry. He wanted the deal to go through because he was set to be the mortgage banker from start to finish. He was enthusiastic but guarded. In all the time I had known Bryan, and through all the deals we had done together, I had often marveled at his ability to develop a strong opinion on a topic without feeling the need to express that opinion. I had always known him to be religious but our conversations had rarely dipped below the surface, so I assumed his position to be that of a live-and-let-live Episcopalian. Frank Mercer, a designer of mostly commercial projects and the architect of record, had driven in from his recently adopted hometown of Asheville, North Carolina. I knew that only because I had spoken with him a week earlier and e-mailed some initial design and concept ideas in hopes that he might sketch out some of the ideas we would be discussing. He had readily agreed and had, in fact, arrived that morning with an armful of sketches and an easel. Lawrence Hill had arrived alongside Dan Richards. Though he didn't carry a Bible and he rarely spoke, I had the unmistakable sense of his awareness of his special hold on the ear of Dan Richards. Lawrence Hill had mastered the art of combining outward humility and absolute confidence. It seemed understood that his would be the final word on Biblical interpretation. He began our meeting with a brief prayer.

"Father," he began, "we just come to you today, knowing that in your unconditional love, you will find favor in the task set before us today. We just ask your blessing as we explore your word in hopes of bringing all the world to know you better. We just ask this in the name of your son, our Savior Jesus Christ. Amen."

"Thank you Pastor Hill," Jason said from his seat at one end of the table. "Can't think of a better way to start this meeting, and I appreciate your help. I also want thank everybody for making the trip. We'll keep it short and sweet, but I think we've got some pretty exciting stuff to talk about today. We're going to talk a little while, see some pictures, eat a little food, and try to get our minds around the wonderful opportunity emerging before us. It's going to be an extraordinary complex with a very simple story, so why don't we let Chad tell us all about it."

"Thank you, Jason," I said, standing and moving in the direction of the display boards. "As Jason said, ours is a simple story, one that begins in the Garden of Eden and invites visitors to witness the splendor of God's creation from the very beginning. I see this as an atrium space, lots of trees and blue sky peeking through, establishing a welcome sense of beginning. Adam and Eve are present, as is the tree of knowledge, and storyboards establish the timeline of original sin and the consequences. Once through the atrium, visitors are encouraged to choose their own path, exploring the Old or the New Testament. Most visitors will choose a chronological path, but we might anticipate repeat visits and allow for those with special interests."

I pulled the cover off of the first display board and revealed Frank's sketch of the atrium concept, canopied and bright. Rather than looking at the display, I tried to read the eyes of those of the table. There was a pensive enthusiasm.

"Are we thinking there will be guided tours?" Jason asked calmly, as if opening the gate for questions. "I hadn't really thought we would need them. I was viewing this more as a family destination with moms and dads leading the charge. More like a Six Flags than a museum." The strategy worked. Dan Richards opened up with his first bit of commentary.

"I think we might reserve the possibility of guided tours," he said scanning the table. "If anything, I think this might be a great opportunity for young pastors to engage in mission-type work with our visitors, building people skills and greater familiarity with our foundational stories." Lawrence Hill gave a nod in support of such an idea, though he didn't speak. I began to wonder if the man was mute, but I continued with the story.

"As we step into the Old Testament, our journey begins with Noah's Ark, a technological smorgasbord that features holograms of animals boarding the ark and living within its walls, ocean sounds and even piped in breezes, closing with the arrival of robotic doves bearing olive branches. This particular display is housed in a multilevel static environment so that visitors experience the upper decks as well as the lower."

"Will any of the animals be built to scale," came the question from Frank Mercer. "I meant to ask you that last week but forgot. The difficulties with that are obvious, but if you envision a multilayer or multi-floored exhibit, the possibilities begin to expand."

Here Jason Sharp interceded, and I was thankful. I had anticipated that some of the questions would involve levels of detail that were beyond my scope, and this was one of them. My task was really the narrative, the story that connected the displays and rides. How those displays and rides functioned individually and collectively were the business of others, allowing me the opportunity to dream up an idealized version of the experience without the baggage of reality.

"We have hired a specialist in amusement displays and interactive animatronics," Jason replied, "one that spent some time in Orlando swampland, so we anticipate his participation will be a vital component of each venue design. At this point, we are really laying out a map of the overall experience, trying to maximize the land use. We will return to a more micro perspective once we get the general layout. That will be a question to address at that point."

"Another central feature," I continued, "at the beginning of the Old Testament side of things is an element I'm calling, for lack of a better phrase, Commandment Corner. It includes a fountain-like depiction of the burning bush, a visual that is at once vibrant and green and then consumed in flame, only to repeat the cycle indefinitely. An additional element of Commandment Corner would be an invisible stone carver, some sort of compressor mechanism with a sandblasting arm and clear hose, that replicates the inscription of the Ten Commandments along a similar cycle." Part of me thought these ideas would fall on deaf ears, that nobody could envision these sorts of venues as even remotely entertaining for anybody. In the back of my mind, I thought for sure there would be too much smoke and mirrors for the ardently faithful. But the response around the small conference table seemed open and receptive, as if the hokey nature of what I was describing stopped short of their years.

"Maybe we can even have small stone tablets in the gift shops," Hill offered with enthusiasm, "like customized license tags for bicycles, with the most popular names already etched in them. So the kids take home a personalized set of commandments."

"We have hired a merchandising specialist," Jason Sharp said quickly, trying to keep the tour on track, "with years in the Christian gift shop and book trade, so she will have a better handle on those possibilities. I am making a note of that idea, though, and will pass it along to her this afternoon. Tell us about the rides, Chad."

"Well," I said, flipping the storyboards to the first ride, "the first is perhaps a centerpiece for the older kids. It is a log ride. We call it Holy Moses, and it incorporates a number of the Old Testament narratives. The ride begins in the bulrushes and climbs to the top of Pisgah, allowing the riders a great view of most of the park or the promised land. From there it descends into an underground theater of sorts where we present Pharoah, the plagues, and the golden calf. Then we climb back up with Moses to talk to God and receive the Ten Commandments with a final descent into the Red Sea, where log rides usually create huge waves and get everybody wet."

"That ought to be really fun on a hot summer day," Dan Richards said with a smile, but how does that play in the winter, since we are going for year-round attendance?"

"Well," I replied as if he had teed the ball up for me, "I'm really glad you asked. The final leg of the descent, at least as I envision it, will be built over a quick-drain vault and enclosed by a double-walled tunnel of plexiglass. In the warmer months, the log itself will part the Red Sea and the water will circle all around the inside of the ride. As temperature dictates, the final descent will trigger a rapid drain of the water, even though from the top of the ride the guests will see only the water below. As they approach the bottom of the ride, the water drains out and is pushed through the area between the walls of the plexiglass tunnel that surrounds them, while braking mechanisms rise from beneath the logs to slow and stop them."

"Oh, Lord," Richards said almost under his breath, "that sounds like a lot of moving parts."

"It is, Dan, but the engineers will make it work or we'll redesign it," Sharp replied confidently. "We dislike litigation as much as the next guy." He then looked my way as if urging me to continue.

"For the purist, there's Heaven & Hell, a more traditional roller coaster that climbs high and descends beneath the ground into a series of vignettes similar to Dante's Inferno. I see very disquieting and rapid stimulation beneath with more beatific and comfortable above, though there will need to be some loops or corkscrews or some other jolts of excitement to keep Heaven interesting and attractive for the youngsters."

There were no responses or questions. The group still seemed hung up on the engineering of the log ride, and the roller coaster seemed vanilla in comparison.

"Then there's the Dark Night of the Soul," I continued, "a spin-off of a popular ride when I was a kid."

Dan Richards looked around the table to gauge the response of the others. He seemed unsure of the direction I was heading. Lawrence Hill seemed to notice and offered up a question as if on cue.

"The name seems a bit daunting, I mean for a kids ride. Don't you think?"

"Well, here's the thing," I replied, moving my eyes between his and Dan's, "this ride will imitate the 40 days of temptation and wandering, when Jesus was unsure. Also the experience at Gethsemane. It is a centrifuge ride."

"A what?" Hill asked quickly.

"A centrifuge. A spinning cylinder where the floor drops away as centrifugal force holds people to the wall."

"You sure that's safe?"

"The technology has really improved, from what I've read, and it fits with the larger story. The ride begins with Wagner's Flight of the Valkyries playing at full volume. It creates a chaotic representation of our hectic lives, especially as the floor begins to drop away and people sense their lack of grounding. Then, a calm voice replaces the music. It is God's voice reading from the Psalms, about fearing no evil and walking through the valley of the shadow of death. Amazing Grace starts up low in the background and builds as the floor rises back up and the cylinder slows to a stop."

"Well, that doesn't sound so bad," Richards said with a smile. "Has a good message at the end and might even scare some folks over to our side, as they say."

"Especially," I replied, "when families have a chance to reflect on the messages behind these rides at the Canaan Cafe, the restaurant that multiplies the loaves and fishes to feed the masses. Or the coffee shop, Altared State, intentionally misspelled to represent the Christian table while also pointing to the essential role of caffeine in parenting." The smiles around the table seemed to indicate general support for the food venues, though I was hesitant, and rightfully so, to introduce Wholly Sheet, my idea for a baked goods venue offering custom sheet cakes and small, square cupcakes. Jason Sharp, after his fourth airport scotch the week before, had suggested with an appreciative chuckle that it was probably better to let that one go.

September 3

It didn't occur to me until I saw my face reflected in her medicine cabinet mirror. How does a man get this far, go to this extreme, rationalize the acceptability of rummaging the pharmaceuticals of a complete stranger? Well, not a complete stranger, but certainly no acquaintance permitted such intimacy. The small shelves held nothing of consequence, nothing of even remote interest, so I closed the mirrored door with a click. That's when my reflection gave me a start. You are a complete jackass, I told myself. But I wasn't listening. I moved on to the small bedroom down the short, carpeted hallway, pushing the door open tentatively despite having seen Agent Wagner's departure a few short minutes before.

The bedroom was still and quiet, the only light coming from the closed but poorly installed vinyl blinds in the lone window. Outside the window I could hear the faint hum of an air-conditioning compressor, the fan beginning to whine like it was about to seize up or throw a bearing. The space where the bed should've been was empty, and the carpet gave no indication or imprint that a bed had ever been present. In its place along the bed wall were scattered shoes, rumpled articles of clothing, and the packaging for a landline phone. The phone itself was closer to the middle of the floor, tethered to the room's only phone jack by a cord that still bore the folds of its recent unpacking. Down the wall to the left was what appeared to be the closet, as some of the overflow clothing seemed to emanate from it. Turning the corner into the closet and hitting the switch with my glove-covered hand, the humming fluorescent tubes slowly broke the darkness. On the racks of metal closet shelving, evenly spaced and organized by color and function, hung a variety of clothing from uniform shirts and slacks to T-shirts and collared golf shirts. On the floor, among the strewn running shoes and flip-flops, several pair of black sneakers and half boots stood out in polished form, neatly situated amongst each other, hoping to avoid contact with the other, less disciplined footwear. I clicked the switch off with a confused shake of my head and took one last look around the bedroom. No furniture. No chest of drawers. No socks or underwear. Nothing to suggest that anyone actually lived here. I checked behind the door and found, beneath the breaker box and the wall, a jog bra hanging from a hook on the back of the door and a short barreled shotgun leaning into the corner, barrel up and chamber open. A closer look revealed a cartridge waiting in the gun's chamber. The bra was red. 34C.

The living room and kitchen were divided by a tall counter, a popular floor plan. The two rooms also shared a chaotic, migratory expression of lifestyle. Like the bedroom, the living area held no furniture. What kind of woman lives without furniture or a closet full of shoes? The floor was, instead, scattered with boxes of personal effects, college memorabilia, and certificates of commendation from law enforcement agencies. The kitchen cabinets were empty, as was the pantry. There were no dishes and no glasses. No takeout bags or pizza boxes. The fridge held 4 cans of Diet Coke and 2 colorful sports drinks.

Not only had the experience been humiliating, I was leaving agent Wagner's apartment without answering a single question. I could only shake my head as I backed out of her door, focused on leaving no trace of my visit, and making as little noise as possible. It was the distinct, metallic sound of a semi-automatic pistol chambering a round that tightened my sphincter.

"Had I known you were coming, I'd have put on a pot of coffee," Agent Wagner said calmly. "And yes, that was a live round being chambered, so you want to be pretty quick about telling me what the fuck you're snooping around for. Armed intruders are shot every day in this city."

"I'm not armed," I said without turning to face her.

"You will be by the time the black and whites get here. Armed and cold. So? You got something to say?"

"I'm sorry. I came here because I need your help and I don't know anything about you," I said, facing the dark green apartment door and the rusty knocker and peephole combination framed by a small metal sticker that read NO SOLICITING. I was, at that moment, feeling especially solicitous.

"Well, you've got a shitty way of asking for help," she said. "Easy to see where your brother gets his people skills. Why don't you turn around real slow and take a seat in that chair there to your left."

I completed all of that and only then made eye contact, my hands resting clearly on the arms of the chair. Agent Wagner remained standing, leaning against the treated post of the small porch without relaxing her grip on the pistol or its full barreled view of me.

"Now, how may I appear to be helping you?"

"I need to know what all Thib has been involved in. What he does with his life is his business, but when it spills over into mine and my family's --" I said, without finishing. It was a weak effort, I know, and Agent Wagner seemed to see right through it.

"Got to do better than that, Golden boy. Remember that I've heard all about you for months now. Concern for your brother's welfare, while quaint, would be a new emotion for you. And what makes you think he's up to anything that affects you or yours, other than that shit with your wife? I'm assuming there's been no subsequent contact with that group. Correct?"

"How do you live without furniture, or even a bed?"

"Stay on message, Chad. Why are you here? Skip ahead to the good part where you go home and I go to work without the hassle of arresting you."

"He mentioned samples from the storage units or something like that. Thib was saying he was involved somehow. Prescription drugs. Not the hard stuff like crack or heroin. Painkillers and such."

Agent Wagner continued to listen with frustration, shrugging her shoulders and waiving the pistol a bit as a result. Somewhere in the distance a lawn crew cranked a blower. "What's that got to do with you and, more importantly, what's that got to do with me?"

"Well, I'm confused. Aren't you the one banging my brother in a climate-controlled storage unit while pretending to be a bartender? Or are you a bartender pretending to be a cop, because the gun and badge look real. I got to give you that."

"While I can categorically deny banging your brother in a storage unit, I am not at liberty to discuss ongoing investigations." Agent Wagner was now emotionless, having entered some state of psychological neutrality that allowed her to both dismiss my provocation and toe the company line. "Unless you have evidence to suggest that any of your brother's talk was true, I can't see where this concerns you, and I recommend you stay out of it. This is not the country club set you seem to have brushed up against. If they have left you alone, take that to the bank. These folks might seem harmless now, but you do not want to fuck with them, even trying to get your brother out of whatever shit he may have stepped in. In the end, you will only increase the body count."

With this proclamation of street wisdom, agent Wagner retired her side arm to its holster and looked between me and the parking lot. The blower in the distance increased its whine to a full throttle pitch before falling silent.

"So unless you know something I don't, I suggest we pretend this never happened and we both get on with the rest of our day."

"My wife's pregnant," I said quietly.

"Well, congratulations," she said with a shrug and a roll of the eyes. I didn't see her roll her eyes, but it felt like she did. Sounded like she did. "I wish you both the best."

"She doesn't know that I know."

"Oh."

"I found a pregnancy test in the trash."

"Well, she's probably just waiting for the right time to tell you. So you can celebrate together. Women can be good at keeping secrets."

"So can men," I replied absently. A breeze picked up and tickled wind chimes in the distance. I looked in the direction of the sound and found the chimes hanging from a tree beyond the rail where agent Wagner was leaning impatiently. "I had a vasectomy about 10 years ago," I continued, punctuating the sentence with eye contact.

"That's awkward. And she knows that?"

"Not that I'm aware of. We've never talked about it. We agreed very early to hold off on children and she's always been on the pill. So it never came up."

"And Thib said this is a second marriage for both of you?"

"Yep."

"Well, that's fascinating, but you'll work it out."

"We have separate bathrooms, so I waited for her to go to work and then took a look around her bathroom and closet."

"I'm beginning to spot a trend," she said with a nod over my shoulder to the door behind me.

"And I found boxes of samples in the bottom drawer of her dressing table, and more in a shoebox in her closet. Mostly Xanax but also Adderall and Oxycontin. All samples, no prescription bottles."

"Doctors prescribe those all the time," she said, now interested but trying to play it off, digging for a deeper connection. "Perfectly legal to offer samples to patients as far as I know."

"True," I agreed, "as long as you're a doctor. But as far as I can tell, Molly hasn't been to a doctor in several years. In fact she's been adamantly opposed to organized medicine for a while. Says that all doctors do is prescribe foreign chemicals that conflict with the body's ability to heal itself. She's big on yoga and supplements and meditation and promoting holistic cures and shit like that."

"But you have no alternative explanation for the meds, do you?"

"That's what makes me rethink what Thib was saying about the storage unit. So I was hoping you could explain what he was talking about." I had used my arms in making the case and was now standing to emphasize the point.

"Sit back down, cowboy," she said quickly and clearly, "this rodeo ain't over yet."

"Sorry," I said, sitting once again.

"If I understand, you are suggesting the possibility that stolen narcotics have made their way into your house, with a possible connection to both Thib and Jeremiah. Correct?"

"Yes, but I have no way to prove it. And even to suggest it might be the end of my marriage."

"Sounds like that's hanging on by a thin thread of DNA at this point, and it's not likely your DNA."

"There is that."

"But here's how you begin the process. Lot numbers. Each box should be stamped with lot numbers and those numbers correspond to manufacturing and distribution data inside pharmaceutical companies. And, sometimes, data gathered by insurance companies when drugs are lost or stolen."

"Okay."

"So go back to your own house and dig around in your own closets and gather data from the boxes you're talking about. If those match the numbers we have uncovered, we can start to ask questions."

"Okay," I said, quickly pushing myself up from the chair while maintaining eye contact. I stepped off the porch ahead of her and began the short walk around the corner of the building to the parking lot.

"I'm assuming you didn't steal anything," she said, joining me on the sidewalk.

"How do you live like that?" I replied without turning to face her. "No furniture. No food. Almost makes the storage unit seem homey."

"Drop the storage unit."

"Sorry."

"And this is more of a safe house," she said, casting a casually purposeful glance around the property. "I really don't have a permanent address, other than a car, I guess. I collect mail at a couple of locations around town and use different addresses, usually removed from the areas I investigate."

"Why is that?"

"In theory," she said, reaching for the handle of her car door, "it keeps the bad people from following me home or rummaging through my closet."

"How's that working out for you, if I was able to follow you back here?" I said with a chuckle.

"Well, I can only assume that you didn't anticipate this conversation today, so you tell me."

As Agent Wagner drove out of the parking lot, I realized that she had made a real impression on me. I couldn't call it sexual necessarily, though she did possess a certain schizophrenic charm as she danced between Calliope the bartender and Agent Wagner the cop. And given what I've heard from Thib about his sexual appetite and exploits, Agent Wagner had to at least pretend to be curious and enthusiastic to hold his attention in bed or storage unit. But she struck me as more than simply sexual, more than the sum of her private parts. She had good sense and a quiet way of controlling the situation, though the loaded gun made a fairly loud statement. The gun and the handcuffs combined brought to mind some interesting role-play scenarios, I admit, but she also seemed interested in and capable of interesting conversation and thoughtful perspectives, but that might have been the adrenaline talking.

At any rate, I got back in my car and waited for my pulse to stabilize and the air conditioning to cool the car down. I thumbed through e-mails and text messages on my phone and pulled through the parking lot and stopped just short of the main road. As the fan slowed and the temperature and noise level in my car were both reasonably lowered, I called Molly.

"Hey," she said cheerfully, "where are you?"

"Looking at a multi--family site close to downtown. How about you?"

"Just wrapping up the tennis team meeting. The girls want to bump up from 3.5 to 4.0 or maybe even form 2 teams, so we've been talking through that."

"Hmmm. Sounds interesting."

"Well they've changed the whole system, so we had to make some decisions. I told them I was going to take a break, let some of the other girls play this year."

"Why's that? I thought you enjoyed the tennis, used it as a good balance to the yoga and all that."

"I don't know. We'll talk about it later. Right now I got to go. I have a showing in half an hour and I need to shower."

"Okay. What have you got after that?"

"Supposed to meet with Angela about listings right after lunch and then my 2:30 Pilates class. Why? What do you need?"

"Nothing," I replied, running the clock face through my line of sight. "Let's catch up at dinner."

"Sounds good."

September 5

"So you were snooping around in her closet," Randy Wilkerson asked, "looking for something, but you don't know what, exactly?"

"Yep."

"And this was the FBI chick or your wife?" he continued, "because I'm getting these stories confused."

He had leaned over his bike and propped his head on the saddle, trying to catch his breath. The last climb up a stretch of particularly steep singletrack had us both feeling our age but equally grateful for the close proximity of good mountain bike trails. We tried to ride every week or so, but schedules lately had been tight and riding time nonexistent. The fluffy clouds set against the deep blue sky had rendered a siren call of sorts on this day, and we agreed that we could both use a break. We hit the trail with pent-up enthusiasm and pushed ourselves harder than we probably should have.

I'd eased into the conversation as we'd readied the bikes at the trailhead, and Randy had expressed his usual concern that my life was more fucked up than usual, probably more than the average therapist would be able to reconcile. I'd only shared bits and pieces, though, and Randy was having trouble connecting the players with the action, and trouble breathing. I was hesitant to share too much, but Randy had demonstrated the great capacity to shred information internally, wipe it out of his memory completely unless prompted for specific details. This made him a good confidant and sounding board.

"A little of both," I said, leaning against a small oak tree with feet still clipped in to the pedals, the tree in one hand and a water bottle in the other. "I was trying to find out more about the agent to see if I could trust her with the stuff I found in Molly's dressing table."

"The prescription drugs."

"Yep."

"And you think your brother is involved somehow," he asked, climbing back onto his bike and clipping in.

"Yep."

"I think I'm starting to get it now," he said, pushing off and starting down the trail ahead of me, presumably to set the pace a little slower.

This section of trail was very technical, but the short climbs were met faithfully by sliding downhill runs and banked switchbacks. The designer and developer of this trail system had made effective use of the terrain, and the ride took on a roller-coaster feel with heavenly open rollers and hellish dashes through stands of trees barely separated by a handlebar's width. We rode about eight minutes before reaching a junction. Randy stopped.

"That's good shit right there," he said. "They've done some work on those switchbacks. Tightened them up."

"It has a nice pace to it. Minimal climb if you work the downhills."

"So has your wife had surgery or anything that might call for meds? Because she seems fit as a fiddle to me, and you said she plays tennis all the time."

"No," I started to explain, holding a small oak and running the pedals backwards to keep my knees from freezing up. "And yes, she plays a lot of tennis."

"So these are not prescribed meds," he continued, catching his breath, "at least in the usual sense."

"They were not prescribed for her, if that's what you're asking. And you don't have to tiptoe around anything. Nobody out here but us."

"Just trying to understand things before I remind you just how fucked up your life really is. I mean, I've never met any government spooks, and I've smoked my share of grass. You're clean as a whistle and you got 'em climbing into your car while your brother's running with thugs and your wife's running the drugs. Hey, see what I just did there?"

"Yes. Very clever, but not very helpful," I replied, sinking my cleats into the pedals and pushing off, setting a slightly faster course for the next run. By the time we'd reached the next junction, following a steady climb over the ridge of the trail system, I decided to stop for a short rest and a snack before heading down a faster, more treacherous stretch. A couple of minutes later, Randy reached the top and dismounted, leaning his bike over in the dirt.

"I'm getting too old for this shit," he said, looking at the trail map framed on the roofed board behind me before coming to rest on the trail bench beside me. "You got another one of those," he said, pointing to the energy bar in my hand.

"Nope," I replied, offering him the last bite of the one I had.

"Probably a good thing. They taste like ass, anyway."

"At the bottom of the hill, maybe, but they taste like prime rib after climbing up here to the top."

"Yeah, yeah. Kick me while I'm down."

This point of the trail system served as an intersection between the bike trail and another trail reserved for hikers. As we sat there waiting for Randy to catch his breath, two hikers emerged from the woods in front of us and paused at the map to check their location. We exchanged pleasantries with the young couple, establishing that it was a gorgeous day and great to be in the woods. They drank from their water bottles and shared an energy bar before heading off.

"I hope they get poison ivy in some hard to reach places," Randy said, turning to watch them walking down the trail behind us. "Did you see the legs on that one?"

"I did," I replied, "but I was more interested in the girl."

"Very funny," he replied, taking a long draw from his water bottle. "So, have you and Molly talked about the meds?"

"No. She doesn't know that I know. I found the pills when I was looking for the pregnancy test."

"What? Are you having a kid, too?"

"It seems likely that she is," I replied carefully, "but I'm not certain that it involves me."

"Is that a politically correct way of saying that there might be a Baby Daddy involved in this somewhere? Because," and here he paused for clarity, "since you've said I don't have to tiptoe around this," and here I nodded in affirmation, "I have to tell you that this tale of woe is starting to take on a serious trailer park texture to it. Remember, I lived through the first wife debacle with you, so I was hopeful when Number Two seemed emotionally stable and comfortable in her own skin."

"Apples and oranges," I replied. "No comparison. And Number One was very comfortable in her own skin. Still is, from what I hear. She just wasn't very comfortable with me there, especially after I stopped preaching. That seemed to have been important to her."

"I remember that. She held on long enough to see if you would go back to it, I recall. Even tried to get me to talk sense into you."

"Really? I never knew that."

"I've tried to put it all behind me," he said. "She was a strange bird."

"She had certain appetites."

"I have no doubt about that. I was always nervous to be in the same room with her and my wife. Very sexual."

"She had it figured out, but I didn't fit the plan."

"What about Molly?" he said, probably trying to keep me from getting back on the bike and heading down the hill. "She got a plan? Because you're saying you might not be the father, and it sounds like she's about to become a statistic."

"I think it's safe to say that I'm not the father."

"Come on, now. It only takes one time."

"And a biological miracle, if there is such a thing."

"How's that?"

"I got snipped about ten years ago, shortly after Number One flew the nest." I stood up from the bench to stretch my legs before getting back in the saddle.

"No shit?"

"No shit," I replied, stowing my water bottle in its cage and beginning the process of getting going again.

"Maybe, in light of that, she's medicating against the conversation she doesn't want to have. I mean, what pregnant woman wants to tell her husband he's not the father?"

"One that marries a man who doesn't reveal the medical impossibility of him fathering a child."

"So she doesn't know?"

"Not that I'm aware of. We never talked about it. It never came up."

"Never came up?" he replied with a chuckle. You're married, for Christ's sake. Most married people talk about shit like that."

"Yeah, well, we never have," I said, clicking into the pedals and beginning the descent through the woods to the parking lot about five miles down the trail.

"Another Springer moment," Randy yelled from the top of the hill.

I reached the parking lot and was almost finished racking my bike and changing clothes when Randy lumbered in. He was scratched from head to toe and breathing hard. His helmet has a sprig of some leafy plant coming out of the top.

"You take a tumble?" I asked.

"I went yard sale off the back of blood rock," he replied, leaning his bike against his car. "Thanks for leaving me for dead."

"Anything sticking out?"

"Not that I can see or feel."

My cell phone chirped and I reached into the front seat of my car to retrieve and answer it. The Caller ID read Private Line, but I had a hunch.

"Chad Felder," I said in a business tone.

"Very official sounding," Agent Wagner said in quick reply. "You got any time left in your busy schedule this afternoon?"

"For you, always."

"Starbucks in 45?"

"See you there."

Randy was hoisting his bike onto the roof rack of his car and pretending not to listen. He wasn't doing either of those things with much success.

"Molly?" he asked without looking my way.

"Agent Wagner," I replied, not looking his way.

"She's the closet, right?"

"And the gun on the front porch, yes."

"You two seem to have gotten past that, if the tone of the conversation is any indication."

"Don't go there," I insisted. "She was pretending to be my brother's girlfriend, and that's out of bounds. Even for me."

"Maybe so, but the question remains, is she good looking?" I paused to consider the question, smiled, and then started the car in the direction of coffee.

"The answer to the short question is yes." Agent Wagner reported the news as Cronkite might have, keeping a distance and objective perspective as she spoke of narcotics I found in Molly's dressing table. "The lot numbers you gave me match numbers we have in our database as reported stolen." She opened the top of her Grande latte and stirred the foam before finishing the thought. "The answer to the question I think you're asking, though, is more difficult. These lot numbers were among others reported stolen from a storage facility up near Cartersville, on the other end of town from the complex Thib has befriended.

So a direct connection to him or through him is more difficult to make than you might have imagined."

She spoke freely from her perforated metal chair in front of Starbucks, her cup atop a matching metal table. She hadn't seemed to carry a purse and was cleverly concealing a gun if carrying one at all. I had initially considered this Starbucks a bit too public. I knew little of the human traffic, despite living less than three miles from the strip mall behind us. I had leased a few of the spaces, but I didn't know any of the employees who served as those companies' boots on the ground. While I feared someone would recognize me and wonder why I was sitting with a strange young woman, I eventually found comforting solace in the reality that I didn't even know my own neighbors, much less the tens of thousands of others who comprised the desirable socioeconomic range needed to develop this site in the first place. I looked out across the generous traffic count passing through the landscaped intersection and tried to connect my brother with a storage unit in Cartersville. It wasn't working.

"Regardless of how they got there, stolen drugs found their way into my wife's dressing table."

"That much appears to be true," Agent Wagner said, putting the top back on her paper cup and adjusting the cardboard insulator. "And while Thib may not be involved specifically with those boxes, he certainly knows your wife and, from what you've said, something about the black market activity around the drugs. So there's a high probability of connection, an argument to be made to keep looking if you have the stomach for it.

"Do you think Jeremiah might be involved?"

"Has Thib mentioned his name in connection to all this?"

"No, but he hasn't said that Jeremiah's not involved, either."

"Ah. The logic of lawyers and English majors."

"Well, it might be worth asking some questions, if nothing else."

"If your logic about Thib is right, Jeremiah has the potential to answer some questions. But I'm not convinced the risk you take is worth the reward you seek."

"I'm not talking about me asking the questions. I'm talking about you. Isn't that your job?"

"We have no official reason to talk to Jeremiah about drugs or his connection to Thib. No probable cause, as they say. We can officially link Jeremiah with Thib at this point, and to stretch what we have puts our larger interest in Jeremiah at stake."

"I don't know what all that means," I said after a familiar-looking woman in the exercise uniform of the modern era walked by stirring an iced coffee, "but I'm at a loss for how I'm supposed to ask a crooked preacher or bishop or whatever his official title is whether or not he's the one giving my brother drugs illegally."

"You speak that church language, don't you?"

"Past life. No longer relevant."

"He sure seems to think it's relevant. You ever listen to him talk? It's like gangster hip-hop with Christian pop song lyrics. Almost comical, if it wasn't so strange."

"He's just using the church to steal from innocent people."

"Oh," she replied with a smirk, "so you prefer the cloak of naïveté when looking back on your decision to leave the ministry for the bricks and mortar world of evangelical capitalism." Her arms extended outward in a crucifix as she almost chanted the last of those words, her hands almost framing the Starbucks logo and the side of the strip mall beyond. "And you prefer to see yourself as fallen when compared to your ministerial peers, because that helps you ease the guilt you feel for making a living instead of doing the Lord's work you felt originally called to."

I began to shake my head in denial but was held in check by the absolute accuracy of her statement. I couldn't help but wonder what Thib had shared with her, and my expression probably gave that away.

"Don't worry," she said, returning her hands to her latte, "none of that was aimed at you personally. I've been around enough crooked preachers to recognize a trend, and to exaggerate that trend to make a point. And for the record, they're not all black and charismatic with a fondness for bling, so I'll save you the trouble of that stereotype."

"That's not what I was saying."

"Like that guy that ran the big Baptist church out here somewhere, with mountain or something like that in the name."

"Mountaintop Baptist?"

"That's the one."

"A friend of mine just listed that entire campus, and four acres to go with it," I said, leaning closer across the table anticipating a good story at a low volume. "I never got the back story, though. The lead minister died unexpectedly and there was some sort of scandal. But I never heard what happened. I assumed the minister ran off with some money and then killed himself."

"Not exactly," she replied, not leaning in and giving no indication that she was dealing in gossip or hearsay. "I think the money walked out after the preacher terminated himself."

"That seems odd. Were you assigned to the case?"

"No, but I remember when it washed through our office, only briefly, when the congregants first suspected foul play."

"Oh."

"That was before all the details were released, though. There was no foul play to speak of." At this point she lowered her voice and took a cursory glance around before returning her gaze to mine. "Unless you think it foul to discover a man of God who has choked himself to death sporting two wetsuits and a big black dildo up his ass."

"Two wetsuits?" I asked, wide-eyed. "What the fuck?"

"Because one is simply not enough."

"No possible way."

"I'm a cop," she replied without expression. "I have no imagination, by design. I couldn't make that up even if I tried."

"Damn," I replied, sitting back in my chair trying to cast that image in my mind and out at the same time.

"Worst part is," she continued, "his wife, who had been out of town at the time, was called back to identify the body and collect his personal effects."

"Damn."

"She left the morgue with her husband's wedding band and a big black dildo in a Ziploc bag. They had to cut the wetsuits off of him."

I couldn't think of anything to say. I could only shake my head in wide-eyed disbelief.

"And he was white as the driven snow. So don't let this little detective game you're playing turn into a racial thing. And never underestimate the sick shit humans do, even when, or maybe especially when, the world thinks the Lord has tapped that human on the shoulder."

"That's all fine and good," I replied, "but you still haven't told me how or why I have to be the one playing this little detective game."

"Look," she said, standing and gathering her coffee cup and cell phone, "you're the one trying to connect the dots. I can see where you're trying to get, but you've given me nothing to work with. I'm not throwing two years of work on Jeremiah under the bus because your wife has a thing for stolen prescription drugs. Nothing in our file suggests that he is involved in this. But you've got my attention now, and when you get more answers you'll have more of my attention. Until then, I can only thank you for the latte and be on my way."

I stood as she began to turn toward her car, but I didn't say anything as she walked away. I did watch, though. And my watching did not go unnoticed. She looked back over her shoulder and smiled. Well not a smile, exactly. More like a don't even think about it. I'd seen that look a million times, and it had never kept me from thinking about it. And that was before you factored in my largely sexless marriage to a woman currently using stolen prescription drugs and carrying another man's child. All told I should probably have chased Agent Louisa Wagner down and cuffed myself to her wildest dreams. But she had admitted to no imagination, and if I knew anything, I knew that sex was a lot like dinner with the in-laws: a little enthusiasm goes a long way.

September 6

As I pulled into the parking lot of my office, I struggled against the involuntary glance toward the dumpster and the thankfully empty spaces next to it. My shoulders relaxed almost immediately and the prospects of a good day were descending upon me when I pulled into my usual spot across from the entrance and took a look in the rearview mirror. On the bench in the landscaped smoking area was Thib, pulling a final drag on a cigarette before dropping it into the ashtray next to the bench. By the time I got out of the car and across the lot, Thib was standing and grinning sheepishly.

"Didn't know you smoked," I said, pausing without actually extending an invitation inside. I hoped we could conclude our business in the smoking pit.

"Haven't in a long while," he replied. "Just started back."

"Well, I would remind you that cigarettes will kill you, but you seem to be outpacing the cancer potential with other lifestyle choices, so I'll skip that part."

"I appreciate that."

"Let's skip all the pleasantries as well, so jump ahead to the part where you tell me what you want."

"I just wanted to apologize," he said with a hint of his characteristic sincerity, Dennis the Menace and Forrest Gump rolled into one.

"Noted and excepted," I said without hesitation or commitment. I'd heard it all before and, quite frankly, had bigger fish to fry on this day.

"And I needed to ask you a question about mom," he continued, "well, really about mom and Janine."

I could only look through Thib to the building beyond and the office and the desk and the foam and the stack of pink message slips under Mildred's Bible where she had begun keeping them for me since we began the theme park project. For her the irony was more than palpable. It was prophetic. I knew there would be a stack of slips.

"Can it wait?" I asked, almost leaning into the door. "I've got a lot on my plate today and really need to focus on me right now. I know that sounds selfish, but–."

"I think I know who the jackal is," he said calmly.

"What? What are you talking about?"

"Come on, Bro," he said with an expression of absolute confidence that I knew exactly what he was talking about. "The note Mom left, at the house? The one you and Dad never showed me."

"Well," I replied, shaking my head more out of curiosity than confusion, "refresh my memory. If I never showed you a note, how do you know there was one and what it might have said?"

"You are such a transparent dumbass. I know the note exists because I have it. I know what it says because I've read it, over and over again, to make up for the years of wondering what the fuck happened when you and Dad went all 'Tarbaby, he don't say nothing' to little brother' when we were little." He could tell that I was preparing to mount a defensive. "And before you ask where I got it, don't forget who helped you move into that fancy gated community of yours. So keep a grip on your righteous indignation."

He pulled out a new-looking pack of cigarettes and fumbled one out and lit it. He looked around the parking lot, exhaled his first generous pull, and then turned back to me.

"Which is worse, preacher man, stealing from your brother what is already his or bearing false witness about events and explanations that defined our childhood? At least my childhood."

"We were trying to protect you from something we couldn't explain."

"Sounds like you were protecting yourselves, but I'm not here to dredge up your old mistakes. I'm just trying to make sense of what is, for me, new information." He took another long pull on his cigarette and blew the smoke skyward.

"If I could explain it," I replied quietly, "don't you think I would've done so by now?"

"Actually, no. I don't. Though I don't blame you entirely for that. You inherited our father's fear of confrontation. I seem to have missed that gene."

"I think we can agree on that last part, though I don't think I fear confrontation."

"Whatever," he replied pushing forward. "Not worth discussing at this point." He took a final drag on a cigarette before dropping it into the ashtray. "Let's take a ride. I've been sitting here a long time."

"I really need to --."

"Won't take but a second, as far as you know. Besides, we don't need to hang our family laundry out here in your own yard."

"But I really don't know anything about the note or the jackal or any of that."

"But maybe I do. Ever think of that? And maybe you should hear it and see it and touch it."

I turned to face the door and the pink message slips beyond before turning back to Thib. I had no interest in following him down this rabbit hole, but I probably owed him a little latitude, having kept the suicide note from him for all these years.

"Okay, but make it quick. This day is disintegrating rapidly."We walked back out to my car and, once settled and underway, headed into traffic making its way toward the perimeter and downtown Atlanta. Thib held a small paper sack in his lap and a small black notebook in his hands.

"What's in the sack?" I asked, pointing with my eyes.

"Stuff. I'll get to it, but I have to walk you through this in order. Otherwise you might just think I made it up in some drug-induced episode."

"I look at the world in probabilities."

"I get that. That's why I need you to piece this together the same way I did. I admit I may have fucked some things up. Turn left at the next light."

We turned at the light and traveled several blocks before turning into a small industrial development, warehouse buildings with office fronts, largely occupied by parts distributors and small manufacturers.

"Where are we headed?"

"Pull up to that spot in the corner, under the oak and next to the fleet of small cars." I did as he asked and shut the car off.

"Now what?"

"Now," he said, opening the small paper sack and reaching in, "we begin our tale of woe." He pulled out what appeared to be a plastic bag full of blonde hair.

"What the hell is that?"

"This," he replied calmly, "is hair. Specifically Janine's hair. The ponytail she cut off when she was 12, I think."

"Shit, Thib," I said, looking between his eyes and her hair, "that's disgusting. What the hell are you doing with that? And what else have you got in that bag?"

"I've had this forever. Since she died. I found it in her jewelry box when we got back from the Grand Canyon. It always fascinated me that she could be dead but her hair looked just like it did the day she cut it."

"Yeah. Fascinating. What does that have to do with this warehouse? Have you changed your home address?" Admittedly, a cheap shot.

"This is not a warehouse," he said, using the ponytail as a pointer. "This is a lab."

I scanned the building from left to right and top to bottom, but I noticed no markings other than the street address numbers above the door. There didn't appear to be any activity in the office portion of the front. The blinds were all tightly drawn and there were no people coming or going.

"Looks like they might be closed today," I suggested. "What kind of lab is it?"

"They are not closed, trust me. They work around the clock. 24/7/365. Their specialty is DNA research. When paternity is a question, these folks have the answer."

"How did you find this place, and why?"

"I did some work for a lawyer a while back. His network was down. Turned out to be a bad router. Simple fix but he talked on and on about the money he was making on paternity suits and how it all hinged on this place," he said, again using the hair as a pointer. "As I got to know the guy, I did more work for him, including acting as a courier for his clients, bringing samples to the lab. Along with technology and security stuff like that. Pretty cool dude."

"And what's this got to do with that?" I said, pointing to the pointer.

"They test DNA from hair samples. So I had them test my hair so I could get a look at my DNA. You know. Have it on file."

"What, like your college transcripts?"

"More out of curiosity. And I wanted to see how a female DNA related to mine might look different, so I had them run Janine's as well."

"Damn, Thib. All this testing can't be cheap. You live in my storage unit and satisfy your curiosity in pretty expensive fashion."

"No worries. I swapped the lawyer time for time, more or less, and he ran the tests through like they were court-ordered. I still do work for the guy. That's not the point."

"What is the point?"

"The results. Very interesting." He locked his eyes on mine.

"What's so interesting?"

"Janine's DNA is very different from mine."

"Well," I replied confused, "you said it yourself. Janine was female. There must be a difference. I'm no biologist, but there must be a difference."

"Sure there's a gender difference, at the chromosomal level, but offspring of the same parents share DNA. Otherwise, how would paternity be established.

"So what are you saying, Thib? That the ponytail may not have been Janine's?"

"No. It was hers. I was there when she cut it off. I remember it vividly, down to the choice of rubber band. That's not the issue."

"Then what is?"

"Janine and I did not come from the same parents. That's the issue."

"Thib," I said with frustration, "what the fuck are you talking about? You are insane."

"That is all but certain, but even the insane can't hide from DNA."

"So you're saying—."

"Like the old Sesame Street song, one of these things is not like the other. One of these things is not like the rest."

"So now you assume that you were the tagalong that's not like the rest? Is that it?"

"Not exactly, no. Full disclosure, I also had your DNA run."

"What?"

"Yep. I told the lab you were killed in Iraq but you had sent our mother some of your hair when they shaved it off at boot camp."

"That doesn't even make sense. I'm too old to have served in Iraq. I never served at all. That doesn't even sound legal."

"Legal, probably not. Compelling, without question. Also slipped a bag of weed to the tech."

"Oh, that's comforting. Potheads in lab coats. And how did you get my hair, anyway?"

"The brush in your bathroom. You should really clean that from time to time."

"Do us both a favor. Jump ahead to the part that doesn't involve me being violated in some way."

"Relax, Bro."

"Don't say that. We may not even be related."

"Nope. Not a chance. You and me are keepers. The differences in the DNA are discernible but expected between offspring of the same gender."

"Oh joy."

"I knew you'd be excited to hear that."

"So Janine may have grown out of a different experience. We have no reason to bring up foul play at this point. All the players are dead. We should let the mystery die with them." Saying this, I reached to turn the key in the ignition and start the car. Thib responded before I could put the car in gear.

"This is the part where it gets interesting." I looked back at him and eased the car into reverse.

"I think I've had enough interesting for now."

"Well, again, full disclosure, I had some pretty strong reason for all the DNA testing, going all the way back."

"I don't doubt that for a minute," I said, looking back over my shoulder and pulling the car back into the flow of the parking lot. "Now whether those were good reasons or rational decisions is a different matter. As for me, I've got a lot of work to get through and you obviously need more help than I can give you."

"I think the jumper was actually Janine's biological father."

"Not what I was expecting," I replied, throwing a glance in his direction, "but I have to give you extra credit for creativity. You see something like this on Springer or did you come up with it all on your own?"

I thought to myself that Randy Wilkerson was going to love the newest wrinkle in the Felder family saga.

"Remember, I said strong reasons."

"Who can forget that?"

"I got to thinking," he continued, "after I found mom's suicide note and realized that there were a lot of unanswered, even unasked questions from Janine's death."

"Such as?"

"Like, why her? Why then? Why did it have to happen in front of all of us?"

"Because the guy was a sick freak," I replied in answer to the series of questions. "That seemed to answer all of those questions at the time. That's not good enough for you, though." I had turned the car back into fairly heavy traffic and found it a struggle to focus on the driving and the apparent stupidity of my own blood brother. DNA was a fickle mistress. "You should leave it alone."

"So I called the Sheriff's office in Coconino County, Arizona."

"Naturally."

"And they were able to dig up the file and the box of related material in a storage unit. The clock had run out and the files in that unit were awaiting shredders and fires. So the nice lady in that office, when I told her I was trying to answer these questions about my sister's murder, said I could come look through the files and boxes before they destroyed them. So I did."

"You went back to the Grand Canyon? When?"

"Last year when I did some convention work in Vegas."

"Convention work?"

"Capturing content. Audio and video of convention seminars and lectures. I think it was orthopedic surgeons, but I don't really remember. I only did the one convention. Boring work."

"Imagine that," I replied, closing my eyes and shaking my head. "But you saw detective work as a promising career field?"

"Turned out a whole lot better than I thought. I really didn't expect to find anything. I mean, if the investigation got nowhere back then, I really assumed I would be disappointed and that would be the end of it. But then I found this note," he continued, reaching into the paper sack and pulling out what appeared to be a scrap of paper.

"From the evidence file?" I said, looking incredulously between Thib and the road ahead. "You stole evidence from the file?"

"They were going to burn it anyway. The nice lady as much as told me I could have whatever I wanted."

"As much as told you or told you?"

"You're missing the point, Chad. Stay with me. I found this note in the file. Apparently," he continued, "this was found in the jumper's front pocket."

"Okay. What's it say? Read it to me."

"It says,' I brought her into this world and I can take her out.' That's it."

"That's it. No names. No connections to us. No indication that it was anything other than a freak accident for Janine. Wrong place, wrong time. Tell me there's more to it than that, that the rest is not a figment of your imagination. Detectives are not supposed to have active imaginations."

"Chad, shit! Would you relax? Where is all this coming from? Just let me tell the story and then you can judge."

"Sorry. Go ahead."

"The note is written on an old version of the notepads used by the Biltmore in Atlanta. The old hotel on West Peachtree?"

"I know the hotel. I'm waiting on the connection. That place was shuttered for a long time. When we were younger."

"Exactly, and the remodeled and rebranded version uses a different logo. But somehow this guy had a pad from the late 50s and he kept it."

"Or he found it. In a dumpster. In Hoboken."

"Next, go back into the early photo albums, the ones I never really made it into because mom stopped taking pictures."

"Okay. How far back?"

"1959. The first book of pictures after their wedding book, since they were married in 1958."

"How do you remember all of this?"

"Just go back in your mind. I have all of the photo albums in boxes back at the storage unit, if we need to refresh your memory."

"I don't remember it. Just tell me what you want me to see."

"A picture of Mom and Dad, fresh-faced and smiling, with the iconic Biltmore sign in the background. The date on the back of the photo was May 17, 1959."

"Okay. So they stayed there in 1959. Probably stayed there a lot. So what?"

"Janine's birthday was February 19, 1960."

I squinted my eyes at the road ahead trying to do the math. Fortunately the intersection ahead was slowing under a red light. When I had reached a stop, I turned to Thib.

"And you said earlier that her DNA was different from yours and mine, correct?"

"I did say that."

"But you can't really confirm that this was the guy?"

"I didn't say that. In fact, I think I can confirm that."

"Well, before you do that, let me pull over here and get some caffeine. This is wearing me out."

I pulled into the Waffle House parking lot, put the car in park and took a deep breath. I had been comfortable with Janine's death as a freak accident whereas Thib obviously had not. I had boxed it up and put it on the upper shelf in a series of closets through the years, never wanting to unpack it or even remember that it was there. Even if Thib had figured out this great mystery, what good did it do? Did it move the human ball forward? No. It probably just unpacked some neatly stored history and piled the remains on the stack of chaos I was already shepherding. Lucky me.

"Okay," I opened, coffee in hand and butt in booth, "confirm away."

"Back to 1959. Mom and Dad were not just staying at the Biltmore. The Biltmore was hosting the 1959 convention of the Georgia pharmacists Association." He opened his small black notebook to check dates. "May 14 through the 17th, 1959."

"And the jumper was a pharmacist, too?"

"Nope," Thib said, looking around for some sweetener for his tea. "Not even close. Marvin High, and yes that was his real name, was on the payroll of the Biltmore in 1959, though the IRS reporting does not list the job title."

"And this was in the Sheriff's file? They tracked the guy back to the hotel?"

"Sure, but they had no reason to connect our parents to that hotel 15 years earlier. If the question was asked and answered, the file doesn't reflect it."

"But you think they connected somehow during that time?"

"That seems more than likely. You see the top of the note?" He asked, offering the crumpled paper. It was stained red and faded in the corners at the top. "They say a body all but explodes on impact from a fall of that height. And this note was in the front pocket of his shirt, so it soaked up some of his blood."

"And you're showing me this because?"

"Because I couldn't find his hairbrush or an old ponytail. The lab was able to test the blood stains on this note."

"And?"

"And it matched."

"No doubts?"

"Not according to the guys at the lab."

"The potheads."

"They don't inhale."

We sat in the comfort of our booth as the past connected around us. A woman's frivolous hook up—presumably, to assuage the spousal boredom of the convention hotel—with a man she may not even have recognized 15 years later. The union produced a child and eventually a pointless sacrifice.

"But there are no other connections that might fill in the gaps over 15 years? No letters or anything like that?"

"Hell," Thib replied, "I'm the youngest. I was eight when she died. I remember her death and Mama's, but there aren't any letters or notes in the boxes of their stuff. I have all of that shit in boxes. And I don't remember any memories of our childhood before that to speak of, so a nuanced visit by an "uncle" or some other person pretending to be a family member wouldn't have meant shit to me. So I got no idea. How about you?"

"Just the Coke bottles."

"What?"

"The only thing I remember that might go back further than your memory is the Coke bottles in the bushes and on the back steps and other strange places."

"Never heard that one. What about it?"

"Well, there was something to it, but I never understood it," I continued. "I used to find bottles in the bushes when I was little. You would have been a baby, so no way you would remember. I was probably five or six. When I found the bottles, I would take them in the house and show them to Mama. She would give me a nickel for the deposit and then hide the bottle in the garbage can."

"You're right. That is strange."

"The strangest part is that she kept telling me not to tell Daddy, but I could never really understand why he would have cared about the bottles or the deposit. And I never really saw either of them drinking a Coke at the house, so I couldn't figure out where all the bottles were coming from and how they were landing in the bushes."

"You ever say anything to him?"

"Yeah," I replied, "a couple of times. Once, when Mama wasn't home and I found a bottle lodged in our climbing tree behind the sandpile. You remember that tree?"

"And the sandpile, but only from the pictures. We had moved from that house by the time I was climbing trees."

"Well, I found a bottle in the tree and was completely confused as to how a bottle ended up in a tree, so I asked Daddy about it."

"And?"

"He took the bottle from me and put it on the kitchen counter. Said he was going to ask Mama about it when she got home. They had a fight about it, I remember that much."

"And the second time?"

"It was after she was gone. I think I was in high school or even college. We were sitting at a barbecue joint and I was drinking a Coke from a bottle. I noticed he had not chosen the same drink and it reminded me of their argument and I asked him about it."

"What did he say?"

"He said something like, 'Your mother had an old friend that couldn't quite let go and the Coke bottles were his way of making his presence known.' That statement never really made sense until now."

"Shit. That's creepy. Sounds more like a stalker than a friend. You think we're talking about the same guy?"

"I don't think we'll ever know for sure, but that's already more than I wanted to know, anyway. It's easier to imagine people doing really stupid shit when those people are not your parents."

The chatter of the diner filled the air, the human symphony of scattered lives, smothered by choices, covered with experiences, and topped with the ceaseless march of time. A medley of voices and plates and sizzling meat, led by the chorus of waitstaff and fry cook and accompanied by the mating call of the hungry, offered a curiously appropriate backdrop. Somewhere in this little restaurant full of people, it occurred to me, probably sat a murderer, an illegitimate child, a cheater, a cheated, and a pothead sitting in a corner trying to analyze it all. And here we sat together at the trough, swapping roles of scientist and subject while the human machine was fueled by coffee and bacon. And considering all the evidence presented, how bad could it really be if I was alive, drinking coffee, and enjoying the uniquely human capacity for reason in trying to assimilate the living woes of the dead? Perhaps a new Waffle House theology was emerging, though theology was too strong a word. Nevertheless, the work was seeping into the life, maybe because I was neglecting the work to be bludgeoned with my family history, but it prompted me to invite him to the interpretation.

"What kind of God sets the stage that way?"

"You asking me?" He replied with a smirk. "You're the preacher on long-term sabbatical. I've never really been a fan, you know that."

"But the way you just described all that, essentially that shit that may or may not have defined us, our family, early on, the way that all played out. How could that possibly have had a grand designer?

Who, in good conscience, would or could keep his or her finger on the pulse of that?"

"And if he could or did, why would rational, reasonable humans offer themselves up in blind faith to such a beast? Surely you're not coming to this realization just now," Thib said in surprise.

"No, not really," I replied thoughtfully, "but that coincidence, the timeframe, all of that gets really muddy."

"What do you mean by that?"

"Well, what I mean is that the events you describe, as I knew them before this morning, were the reasons I had for feeling the love of Jesus in my heart, the presence of something larger than us, like a Holy Spirit of sorts."

"Amen to that," the waitress interjected, lifting the coffee pot over the napkin dispenser and menu rack. "I feel the presence of the Lord each and every day. I'm blessed to have him in my life, so blessed." Thib and I looked at each other and then up to her.

"Even when the bad stuff happens?" Thib asked her. Under normal circumstances I would've been anxious about posing such a question, but she had jumped in with both feet and a coffee pot.

"All part of the plan," she replied, "but we have free will to blame for most of the bad stuff."

"How's that work?" he continued.

"Well," she replied, reaching behind her to put the pot back in the coffeemaker, "it's real simple. We are sinners. We are born that way, and we do bad things to ourselves and each other because Satan is fighting for our souls."

"Okay. And free will?"

"We have the choice. We can follow the path of righteousness that Jesus lays before us, or we can fall back into evil ways and bad things will happen. Simple as that." With that, she smiled and turned to pick up an order of scrambled eggs for an obviously hungover man at the far end of the counter, close to the register.

"She's a sweet gal," Thib said after she was out of earshot, "and she obviously works very hard, but that shit doesn't even make sense."

"Does to her," I said looking into my coffee mug like it was a crystal ball, "and that's what matters."

"Whatever gets you through the night."

"Does to a lot of people, actually."

"Doesn't make it right," Thib replied. "Just popular."

"And profitable. I'm supposed to be building a theme park around all that."

"How's that working out for you?"

"I'm so happy I got to witness this morning," the waitress said, returning with a smile and a yellow check. "Does my heart good to share the good news with friendly folks like you. I hope you have a blessed day!"

September 7

I was standing at the bar at the Cincinnati Country Club, looking out the window at the city skyline while waiting for a Maker's Mark and water. A little swing lube to welcome the PM side of the day and the shotgun start fast approaching. Bryan was warming up on the range, but I had promised to bring him a drink when returning to our cart for the start. As the bartender finished up both drinks, a quiet voice walked up behind me.

"Mr. Felder, we're so glad that you could join us."

I turned to greet Lawrence Hill. We shook hands and exchanged the usual greetings.

"Thanks for having us," I replied. "I've been through here a million times, but I've never seen Cincinnati from this angle. Great view."

"It is. It is. Have you met the others in your foursome?"

"No, not yet. I stopped off for the pause that refreshes," I replied, holding up my plastic cups. "Meeting Bryan back at the cart."

"Well," he continued, ignoring the cups, "your playing partners have expressed great interest in your project."

"Our project," I reminded him.

"Yes, well, be that as it may, we may have an opportunity to extend our mission with these folks," he said. "They represent foundations with global reach."

"And they want to build parks like this in other places?"

"I'm not saying that. I'm just saying they've expressed a genuine interest in our mission, and the potential for this project to support other ministries."

"Well," I replied, "we'll chat them up and whip them into a frenzy. Maybe even do some speaking in tongues."

Hill chuckled guardedly, not sure how to take that last part, and I smiled a big smile and made my way to the door with the drinks. I wandered back through the pro shop to the patio and the collection of readied carts beyond where Bryan was putting his putter back in his bag and looking around for me.

"Thought I was going to have to drag you out of the bar, and we haven't even started yet," he said.

"Got sidetracked talking to your preacher friend, Lawrence Hill."

"You swap the secret codes and handshakes they taught you in Bible school?"

"They've changed them since I got out of the biz," I said.

"That figures."

Two men walked up behind us and stuffed clubs back into the bags on the cart next to ours. They were tall men with short haircuts, and their clothes were so freshly creased that it seemed they might've just been purchased in the pro shop. They smiled and extended their hands in introduction. I registered the names and immediately forgot them. I made it a habit, when playing golf with strangers, not to even pretend to remember their names. Bryan repeated their names when introducing himself in a textbook Dale Carnegie maneuver. I celebrated his proficiency with a long sip of my drink. Fortunately for me, their physical features lent themselves to easy nicknames, so in my head I remembered the stocky one with bright orange hair as Red and the other, alarmingly thin one with a noticeable list to the front, as Lurch. We settled into our carts as one of the assistant pros tested the public address system before handing the microphone to a smiling Dan Richards.

"Well, boys, we thank you for making the trip up the hill. I know you'd rather be at the office this afternoon, but we'll try to make it worth your while. First, I want to ask Reverend Hill to lead us to the Lord in prayer."

"Oh gracious Lord," Hill began, having emerged from somewhere behind Richards, "we just come to you today to express our gratitude for this great day and we just appreciate the opportunity for fellowship in the beauty of your creation with the men you have chosen to lead your flock in business and ministry. We just ask, Lord, that you bring these worlds and these men together to the common ground that you create in their hearts as we celebrate the opportunity for ministry in Charlotte and beyond. And we just ask these things, Lord, in the name of your Son, our Savior, Jesus Christ. Amen."

The low murmur of echoed amens was punctuated by high-pitched feedback as Hill passed the microphone back to Richards. I had bowed my head slightly for the prayer but had chosen to scan the faces framed by the open windshields of the golf carts, eyes closed and hearts opened, as they say. What was it about the power of prayer that compelled leaders of business to invoke the divine? If God was blessing them in the good months, was he ignoring them in the bad? If these leaders quantified their business with a balance sheet and managed people and capital according to those concrete numbers, where did the abstraction of a personal God factor in?

"Thank you, Reverend Hill, for those inspiring words," Dan Richards began, "though I think I heard a prayer request from some of these boys about keeping the yips away." There was a chuckle from the group as Richards looked around. "But seriously, we are here today to have some fun and fellowship, so I won't keep you but long enough to remind you of our little project down in Charlotte. Most of the design team is here, so make sure you meet them and ask them some tough questions. Get comfortable with the idea, because we'd love to bring you along on our mission to do the Lord's work. And remember, all the greens break toward downtown, at least as far as you know, and every green has a three putt bucket, so give up a twenty for the local food bank if you can't get down in two. I've played golf with most of you, so I know the food bank stands to collect a small fortune today. See you at the finish line for food and beverage."

And with that we were off to find the 13th tee, our assigned starting point. I drove as Bryan read the rules and began to speculate on the winning score. Even though he'd not played the game for long, Bryan was a fierce competitor and hated the thought of losing.

"What do you think about a cart bet?" he asked, looking back to see if our playing partners were behind us. "These guys look like naked Auburn fans at an Alabama pig roast. I think we can take them."

"Pretty bold statement for a 21 handicap, don't you think?"

"You're the A player," he said, pointing to the scorecard on the steering wheel I was holding. "I'm probably the C or D, according to handicap, but I'm not above you carrying me back around to the 12th hole."

"You're heavier than you think," I replied without looking his way.

"Don't make me come over there," he replied with mock scorn across the short distance of the cart seat. "Chickenshit."

We pulled up to the tee box and readied for the ceremonial shotgun blast and our first drives. Red and Lurch offered to start us off, and they both striped their drives 250 yards down the middle. I looked at Bryan. He said nothing. Instead, he swung mightily at his opening drive and launched a missile over the trees into the neighboring fairway. I followed the others with a drive down the middle and, after a detour for Bryan's second, third, and fourth shots, we all met again on the green.

"You guys played here before?" Red asked.

"Hell," I responded at Bryan's expense, "I'm not sure he's played before at all." This got a laugh. Even a small one from Bryan.

"Well, Dan's right about a lot of things, but the slope of these greens is not one of them. So don't assume they all break toward the city."

"This your home course?"

"No," Red replied, pulling the flag and letting it fall clear of all the expected putt lines. "We're from Columbus, but Dan's been a generous host through the years." Lurch was away and was busy lining up his 40-foot par putt. "How about you two?"

"Atlanta and Greenville," I responded quietly, pointing to myself and Bryan in turn. Lurch left his putt short to the low side. Red lined up his par putt, still outside of my pending birdie effort, but missed the putt on the high side, leaving himself a slippery downhill return. I sank a six-footer for birdie and we all moved on to the 14th tee.

"So how are you two connected to Dan's Folly?" Red asked on the tee.

"Creative and financing," I replied, again pointing to myself and Bryan respectively. "How about you?"

"We've worked with Dan on smaller projects in the past, mostly private equity placements and limited partnerships in emerging markets. Oil and gas, mining, cellular, that sort of thing."

"So you're in the investment business?"

"Asset management, really, because of the variety of opportunities we offer our clients."

"More than just making a buck, I suppose," I responded, the cynicism sliding a little too readily from my mouth.

"Considerably more," Red replied. We had paused as each in our foursome hit their drive, and now Lurch stood poised over his. He hadn't said a word beyond his own introduction, and I began to wonder if his was more the analytical role to Red's more affable sales side of the partnership. When he had struck a second drive down the middle, Lurch picked up his tee and carried the conversation as we walked back to the carts.

"Trinity Asset Management pursues a decidedly Christian agenda on both the client and investment side. We've made a concerted effort to align our marketing and asset allocation strategies to facilitate what we call progressive tithing."

"Progressive tithing? Sounds like a graduated tax structure."

"It's really just a way of saying that, while we put our clients' capital to work in pursuit of the highest possible return, we also try to focus on those opportunities that most closely align themselves with fundamental Christian teachings and our clients' desires to foster God's work in the world."

"Is that like tax-advantaged Samaritanism?" I asked. It was a sincere question, but Bryan sensed the edge.

"Man sinks a birdie putt and now he thinks he knows everything about the investment business," Bryan said as we climbed into our carts. "You boys better hang on. This is going to be a long round."

Fortunately, golf tends to divide conversations into segments, with most of the dialogue occurring on the tee and green. Bryan took our ride down the fairway as an opportunity to assess the situation.

"What the fuck was that all about?" he asked. "You trying to sink this ship?"

"Progressive tithing?" I replied. "Are they serious?"

"That's their business. You don't have to invest with them, so let them worry about what they call whatever it is they do. What does it matter?"

"Whatever."

Meeting again on the 14th green, Red was lining up a lengthy par putt as Lurch made his way over to where Bryan and I were standing, ready to watch the line.

"So how long have you guys been doing this?" I asked quietly, waiting for Red to putt.

"We actually started out together right out of college. We had just graduated from Liberty and were interning in a couple of congressional offices in DC when we developed the big picture idea."

"There's more to it than the investing?"

"Yes. We offer a broad range of services to individual and institutional investors but we also manage assets deployed through venture capital opportunities and political action committees."

"You guys run a PAC?"

"Several. That was actually the start of the firm. It grew out of our internships."

Red missed his putt left and Bryan shot me a sideways glance as he walked to his ball to attempt his par putt, as if he could see where the questions were heading, and he didn't seem to like the direction. Bryan was not one to allow theology to interfere with revenue, and Dan Richards was a whale in his world. I was just the jackass trying to fuck it all up.

"Who are some of the candidates you support with your PACs?" I asked Red, standing on the 15th tee waiting for the group ahead of us to clear the green on the short Par 3 hole.

"We support mostly issues rather than candidates directly."

"Such as?"

"Family values is probably the strongest issue for us, along with pro-life legislation initiatives and First Amendment preservation."

"Abortion and gay rights and prayer in schools."

"Those are certainly some of the biggest issues, yes."

I dropped my ball between the tee markers and moved it around with the head of my 8-iron until it settled on a solid tuft of grass. I hadn't really given these issues much thought in a long while. I hadn't attended school or prayed in years, so I had no real dog in that fight. I had proven to be, in my own estimation, a flaming heterosexual through the years, so beyond the obvious equal human rights argument and a handful of gay friends, I was far removed from the front lines in that battle as well. My connection to the abortion issue had also receded in the past, along with the essential testicular plumbing, but Molly's presumed pregnancy washed that possibility ashore once again.

"And I'm assuming," I said without looking up, addressing the ball and alternating glances toward the green, "that your position on those issues does not favor the individual rights of women, homosexuals, or non-Christian students."

"Just hit the ball," Bryan said with thinly veiled frustration. "A lot less talk and a little more action, cause this conversation ain't satisfactioning me."

I struck the ball to punctuate Bryan's criticism, sending it through the air with a slight draw and landing it about five feet from the pin. I turned and gave him a wink.

"I think we can all agree," Red replied with a grin, "that our positions seek to protect the sanctity of marriage, the constitutional freedom of religious expression, and the right to life of an unborn child. I think we can also agree that these positions are not always popular."

"Okay. So I'm part of the design process for this theme park or God Experience and you boys are potentially part of the money behind it. Correct?"

"That has been suggested," Red replied, planting a tee in the ground and placing his ball on it. "And we are intrigued, on behalf of our clients, by the idea and the opportunity." He gave his iron a mighty swing and we all watched as his ball faded slightly off target and landed in the green-side bunker.

"Okay. So how do you see this investment aligning with the fundamental Christian teachings?"

Bryan sighed and shook his head as he readied to hit his tee shot. Always in favor of talking through his backswing, mainly to get in his head, I further qualified my question.

"I mean, I'm at the beginning of the design phase for the narrative thread that runs through the development, so what can I potentially do to make the design more attractive to you and your clients?"

With a thin sound and an audible grunt, Bryan shanked his tee shot through the trees and into the road beyond. He turned to me with tight lips and furrowed brow.

"Keep it up, my brother," he said as he walked back to the cart and slammed his club back into his bag. This drew smiles from the rest of us as we climbed into our carts. Red and Lurch started down the path and Bryan let them get a head start before easing in their direction.

"What's going on with you?" he asked, watching the cart path and maintaining what seemed to be a safe distance behind the others. "I realize that you have this thing about being the smartest guy in the room, and sometimes you work really hard at it, but you need to cut these boys some slack unless you want to kill this deal for both of us."

"I hear you."

"I don't think you do. It's like you're somewhere else. And go easy on the brown water, because we damn sure don't need it to get any worse."

"I think I'm asking legitimate questions."

"I bet you do," he replied with a glance in my direction, "but your tone has that condescending atheist edge to it, like these guys are idiots. Hell, like I'm an idiot."

"So you think the government should regulate a woman's reproductive health?"

"What the fuck, Chad? We're trying to get through a round of golf with these guys and make nice about a project that makes us a little money. Why does it have to become some cerebral launching pad for your liberal bullshit? Why do you even give a shit?"

"Molly's pregnant."

Bryan slowed the cart to a stop about halfway to the green. The others had reached the green and were pulling their putters out and walking toward their balls. He looked at me with a serious but confused expression.

"Congratulations, I guess," he said. "Though you seem undecided about the prospect of fatherhood."

"Kid's not mine," I replied without expression.

"What do you mean? How do you know for sure?"

"I removed that possibility about ten years ago, after the first go around."

"So what has she told you about it?"

"Nothing. She doesn't know that I know."

"How's that?"

"I found a pregnancy test box one night when the neighborhood dogs got into the trash. The next morning, after Molly had gone to work, I found a positive pregnancy test rolled up in a plastic bag at the bottom of the kitchen garbage can."

"Damn."

"Yeah, damn. You better drive on up to the green before Jehovah's witnesses begin to wonder if you're firing up a joint back here."

Bryan pulled up behind the other cart and we putted out on the 15th and moved ahead to the 16th tee, again waiting on the group ahead to clear the fairway before we could hit our drives. Red teed up and stepped back to wait.

"I appreciate your question and your interest in making the park an attractive investment option," he said, "but I don't know of any ways you could make the experience or narrative more compelling than the Bible itself. For our clients, the Word made manifest in an educational and recreational setting, one that introduces and spreads the Good News, is a great story. So that side of the equation, so long as it remains true to Biblical teachings, falls in behind solid numbers."

"I think," Bryan jumped in, probably fearing my response, "that we can also all agree that the numbers have to work, and the numbers on this are, indeed, quite strong."

"And we can get comfortable with that," Red replied, stepping back up to his tee shot. "Our clients are more interested in positive experiences and the larger restoration of Jesus Christ to his rightful place in our country's governance structure than they are concerned about single issue politics." With a crack he sent his drive sailing well right, almost out of bounds.

"So, from what you're saying," Bryan asked, "is it safe to assume that you see the potential for more than one of these experiences?"

"We do see franchise opportunities, yes," Red replied, "but a lot of that depends on the reception of this first project, and we are cautiously optimistic about that."

"That's more than I can say about your drive," Lurch said, before teeing up his own ball and launching his drive in the same general direction as Red. He shrugged as we walked back to the carts and headed down the fairway.

"Does anything about what these guys are saying scare you?" I asked Bryan as we watched the others drive across the fairway to the extreme right side of the course to hit their second shots.

"Not as much as the thought of my wife carrying another man's child without even telling me about it. What are you going to do about that?"

"I don't really know yet. I mean, it would be really easy to just cut her loose and let her make whatever decisions she needs to make. That would allow her to hold the baby daddy accountable, I guess."

"Almost force her hand on that one, I would think."

"No, probably not. She's got a small trust fund and she's done pretty well in the house business, if that market ever comes back. It wouldn't be easy, but she could make it."

"How long have you guys been married?"

"Four years."

"You guys ever talk about having kids?"

"Not really, but does that even matter at this point?"

"I guess not," Bryan said. "Just trying to understand."

"So am I, Brotherman. So am I."

The rest of the round was a blur, though I managed to carry the group through most of the holes and we scored somewhere in the middle for the tournament. We returned to the clubhouse for drinks and chicken fingers and Dan Richards mingled actively, like a pinball making contact with as many of the bumpers as he could in the time remaining. He was the consummate salesman, smiling and glad-handing across the bluestone terrace like a man running for office. His smile expanded as he approached me.

"Chad," he said with a clap of his hand on my shoulder, "I hear you've been asking some tough questions."

"Just trying to get the story straight," I replied with a smile. "I want you to get your money's worth. Besides, they seemed up to the challenge."

"Indeed they did," he continued, "and seem all the more interested for it. So thanks for that."

"Well, I was sincere with the questions. I'm really trying to capture the essence of what you're after with this project."

"And you're doing a great job," he said. "That must be another of your particular strengths. We've got this idea that keeps growing, and now you're a part of it, even if you didn't necessarily want to be. You probably made some strong decisions about these things years ago, but here you are, wrestling with the ideas anyway, almost like you can't walk away from a challenge or the opportunity it presents to make things right. On some level, it's what developers do. They take situations and pursue the highest and best result. Same with preachers, I suppose. At this point, though, it's a lot like kids. You got kids?"

"No."

"Well, trust me on this one. It's very similar. It's never the right time or the ideal circumstance, but that kid's coming anyway. Whether it's an answered prayer or a complete surprise, soon enough you got boots on the ground. And those boots can walk the right way or the wrong, but they're going to walk sure enough. Just like our little project. It's coming out of the ground and we're going to be there for the birth. Let's just hope we raise it right, that we give it the love it needs and the hope it requires. That's the essence of this project. Hope and love. And you don't have to be a Christian to see that, but it helps." This last part he said with a sly grin as he patted me on the back and bounced to the next bumper on the bluestone.

"Did you tell him Molly was pregnant?" Bryan asked as Dan cleared earshot.

"No, but he picked a spooky analogy."

"Did you see what he just did there? I'd swear he was listening to our conversation right before he walked up."

"Sure seems that way, but I don't know why anybody would. It's my own little train wreck."

"Or Molly's," he countered. "Sounds like your train never left the station on this one."

"Well, you're right about that, but my wife is still pregnant."

"From where I stand, wife and pregnant are mutually exclusive."

"Maybe so, maybe so. And make no mistake, I hear what you're saying. And I like the way you make it sound so simple. I'm just not convinced it is.

September 9

I had circled the main lot twice before giving up and turning toward the adjacent parking deck, on the far side of the hospital from the emergency room. I felt like I'd run a marathon by the time I got to the ER waiting room and nurses' station.

"Molly Felder," I said to the nurse, pointing over her head to the rooms behind her. She checked the computer screen in front of her. Then she checked it again, apparently missing the name the first time that she looked back at me with a confused expression.

"We got a Molly Duncan," she said. "That the one you looking for?"

"That's the one," I said, "married name. Sorry."

"Come around to the side and I'll let you in," she replied without expression.

So I made my way to the side door and tried to remember if our health insurance listed her under my name or hers, or if it even made a difference. Then the door opened and I followed the small, pudgy nurse in what appeared to be Jackson Pollock's scrubs to the end of a series of curtains. Behind curtain number whatever was Molly, resting against a pillow with an oxygen tube around her ears and under her nose and an IV tube sticking out of her right arm.

"Hey there," I said, waking her from what appeared to be a light sleep. "Looks like they're getting you all fixed up." I sat on the edge of the bed and stroked her left arm before grabbing her hand. "You feeling better?"

"I am," she said groggily. "Sorry for all the trouble."

"No worries. I'm just glad you were so close and able to get yourself here. I'm sorry I wasn't closer."

Before she could respond, the curtain swung open on the steel bearings in the ceiling. A doctor and a nurse filled the gap, clipboards in hand. I stood and extended my hand. Introductions were made and the nurse moved toward the head of the bed to record vitals. The doctor flipped through the file on the clipboard.

"Well, the good news," the doctor said without looking up, "is that mother and child are doing fine. Dehydration was the main culprit, and perhaps too rigorous an exercise regimen. But," he continued, now looking between Molly and me, "the IV will fix part, and a focus on prenatal exercises and vitamins will help the other. The bad news, and I'm waiting on some final blood work on this one, is that Molly seems to have competing forces in there somewhere, drugs that shouldn't be taken together because they don't get along, certainly not in the quantities indicated."

To this point I had not looked at Molly. We had never discussed the pregnancy, so she assumed I was learning of it only now. I didn't even know where to begin on the drugs. I continued to focus on the doctor.

"I'm looking at the admitting nurse's inventory and you've indicated that you are taking no medications at this time. Is that true?"

Okay. I had to look at Molly at this point, as she mustered a response to the doctor's question. I kept my eyebrows up and my happy face on, even as my eyes met Molly's. Tears were welling up and I noticed a trail of tears on her cheeks.

"Mrs. Duncan," the doctor continued purposefully, "the information you provide needs to be as accurate as possible. It can mean life or death for you and your baby. So I need to know if you are currently taking any medications."

In hindsight, it was probably not the drug question that stalled the works. Molly was probably still processing the doctor's revelation—one that had only been news to him—and the effect it was having on me. I could only assume that she had been planning to tell me, and this had not appeared in any potential scenarios, even worst-case.

"I have been taking some medicine for my back. I don't remember the name of it. I only take it when the pain gets really bad." She looked only at the doctor as she spoke. When finished she turned back to face the machines, and I began to wonder if maybe the doctor had sedated her before my arrival.

"Well, that's good news," the doctor said. "That explains some of the test results. Gives us something to work with. Mr. Felder," he continued, looking in my direction, "while the nurse is checking vitals, if you'd like I can catch you up on where we are to this point, but we'd need to walk and talk. I need to check on some folks I admitted this morning."

"Okay. Sounds good." I squeezed Molly's hand and tried to get her focus. "I'll be right back, Molly."

We were clear of the ER before the doctor really got down to it. Traces of narcotics in the blood test. Indications of significant doses. Confusion as to why her primary care physician would prescribe such during pregnancy. I tried to respond as if I was as surprised as he was, but apparently I was doing a poor job of that.

"You don't seem surprised," the doctor said, pausing in front of the drink machine near the main lobby, "so I assume you've known about the meds."

"Not that we've talked about," I replied.

"And I've experienced enough pregnancy revelations to have a hunch that you hadn't talked about that either. Correct?"

"That's correct."

"And you know about the child even though she hasn't told you?"

"Correct."

He fished the can from the bottom of the drink machine and popped the top. After a long pull from the can, he seemed to consider the pause that refreshes as if he was wondering where the day had gone. Then, as if he remembered I was standing there, he continued.

"Here's the thing. The lab flagged the toxicology on her because of the combination of substances, so one painkiller, while not a good idea, is only part of the issue. Plus, depending on your pharmacy, somebody should be cross-checking, either the doctor or the pharmacy, preferably both."

He paused. I guess he thought I needed time for it to sink in. Or he was trying to figure out a polite way to say the next part. I, on the other hand, was enjoying his clinical directness.

"Here is the other thing. She had to be sedated a while ago. Not on arrival. Only after the blood was drawn and the nurse started talking about prenatal vitamins and hydration. At that point she became visibly agitated and talking about having to get home and get supper ready for you and stuff like that. Concerns not usually expressed by a woman who arrives in a tennis skirt. I've seen that face before and she was scared."

"I'm not really sure, but are you suggesting she was indicating a fear of me?"

"Look, all I'm saying is that hormones do strange things to pregnant women, and if she hasn't told you about it, there must be a reason. So try to keep a handle on things when you go back in there."

"No worries on this end," I said. "I have a pretty good idea why she hasn't mentioned it."

"Well," he said raising his hands and the drink between us, "that's none of my business, unless you want me to think you are a family and children services risk, and I don't get the feeling you are."

"Correct. I am not. We're all good here."

"That's great news. Now I'll see if the lab can help us on the other substances."

"Try the combination of Xanax and Adderall and see what you get."

The doctor, who had begun to turn away, turned back to face me. He was doing the chemistry in his head.

"Are you in pharmaceutical sales?"

"Nope. Don't have the legs for it. Or the tits." The humor was barely acknowledged.

"Then you've seen these bottles on your vanity or in your medicine cabinet? Somewhere in your life?"

"More or less."

"But those are not painkillers, at least not usually. I don't think her doctor would prescribe them as such. And if you use the same pharmacy, this combination should've sent up red flags."

"I have not been as active in her healthcare as I probably should have been?" I posed, almost as a question, "because I'm not up to speed on the uses or the diagnoses. I've just seen those names around the house." If the doctor doubted me, his face didn't show it.

"Okay," he said, looking at his watch, "well, let's see what the lab comes up with. Until we know for sure, I'm inclined to hold her overnight in case we're missing something."

"Sounds reasonable."

It was difficult to say whether or not it sounded reasonable to Molly. By the time I got back to the room, the sedative had really kicked in. She was in and out of the conversation and mostly apologizing for not letting me know sooner about the baby. I tried each time to assure her that it was not a problem and that the news was exciting and she was glowing. All the usual responses to such announcements, delivered with a confident smile and a compassionate pat on the hand. The hardest part was pretending to be surprised. Eventually she was admitted to the hospital and transferred to a regular room on the 3rd floor. I left to grab a bite and retrieve some of her things from the house.

On the way back to the parking deck, I checked my phone and noted that I had missed three calls, all from Thib. In spite of his apparent urgency, I planned to call him back the following day, at the earliest. That resolution was interrupted by a fourth call from his number, and I decided to get it over with.

"Hello, Thib."

"Hey, bro. What's up?"

"Not a good time. Can I call you back, couple of days, maybe?"

"I just got the strangest call," Thib reported, completely dodging the Dodge. "Jeremiah seems to think you play for him now. Something about a deal you got working. Any of this ring a bell?"

"Just a real estate deal, Thib. That's it. The listing agent is a buddy of mine, and I put Jeremiah's name in the hopper as a prospect. I'm just a referral."

"Are you fucking nuts? These people don't do real estate the way you people do real estate. Have you forgotten our little trip to their home office?"

"What does that even mean? How is there more than one way to do real estate?"

"You just don't get it. Why would you want to have anything to do with him? You jumped my shit for the same thing. Seems hypocritical to me."

"Not the same thing," I replied, trying desperately to hang on to my patience. "Not the same thing at all. Real estate transactions are legal. Your activities are not always so."

"I did nothing illegal to get that data, and what he did with it is his business."

"I'm no lawyer, but it wasn't yours, no matter how you got it. And you're not going to tell me he's not a part of your drug cartel. At least I'm not going to believe it if you do."

"Shit ought to be legalized, anyway. Sending folks to jail for smoking weed is complete nonsense."

"I'm not just talking about the weed," I replied, spotting an opening and thinking of Molly. "I'm talking about the prescription stuff walking around from your own neighborhood."

"I'm not involved in that anymore, I told you. Besides, that stuff's about like weed, temporary fix for what ails you, maybe a little stronger than tequila, but not much. Takes a suburban housewife from carpool to carpool, they say."

"Like Molly?"

"If she drove carpool, maybe."

"That's not the point. Did you ever give any to Molly?" There was a pause, but not as long a pause as I expected.

"A couple of times, maybe," he replied, "when she wrenched her back playing tennis."

"How much did you give her, Thib?" I was now in the parking deck and I became aware of my voice echoing through the rows of cars. I pushed the unlock button on my remote and looked around for the blinking lights. "How much?"

"A couple of samples, Chad. Jesus Christ. Her back was hurting, man. She said they worked. Made her feel better. That was that. End of story."

"Just a couple of samples? To help her back?"

"Yep. No harm no foul, right?"

"Except that I just left her hospital room." I had reached my car and was settling in behind the wheel as he tried to connect the dots.

"Hospital?"

"And the doctor is still trying to figure out what combination of chemicals is swimming around in her bloodstream."

"Is she okay?"

"She will be when they figure out the chemistry, so there's your no harm no foul."

"Shit, bro. That is messed up."

"That your official pharmacological diagnosis?"

I would eventually regret hanging up on him, but it would probably take a while. Sure, I was frustrated and I was tired of his intrusions in my life, tired of constantly cleaning up his messes. At least it felt that way to me. But as I sat there listening to the car quietly idle and the voices softly emerging from the radio, I realized hanging up so abruptly was mostly for dramatic effect. Thib wasn't going to change, no matter how many times I hung up on him or yelled at him or pointed out his tragic flaws. The phone rang immediately and I answered with an apology cloaked in bravado.

"Sorry about that. Your stupidity brings out the worst in me."

"Well, you sure know how to charm a girl," the female voice said through the phone. Instinctively, I held the phone away from my face to check the caller ID. Again, private number. I brought the phone back to my ear.

"Sorry. Thought you were someone else," I replied sheepishly.

"Smart money says I know who that is."

"Probably so. What's up?"

"Well, I hate to throw a wrench into your exciting evening, but I thought you should hear from me that your favorite righteous man is currently being held without bond and it's not looking good. For him anyway. I thought you ought to know. They just picked him up a half hour ago."

"On the drug thing or the other stuff?"

"Other stuff. Way beyond what you were involved in."

"Holy shit. Is that what you been working on?"

"Yep. I'm assuming you didn't have time to ask him any specific questions. We have no indication that he has ever been involved with the prescription drug scene."

"I was just a referral on the church deal," I replied, "but Thib came clean on the samples. That's why I was mad just a second ago. He just called."

"Can we meet and discuss? Some of that sounds like it might match up with new evidence we have. If you don't mind. I can get an administrative subpoena if it makes you feel better."

"Is Thib in trouble to the point he might do time? I mean, now that you have Jeremiah, are you coming after him?"

"We need to talk through some of that and then Thib will have some choices to make. Can you meet me in a couple of hours?"

Later That Evening

The cars in the rearview mirror all started to look the same as I made my way downtown, working against rush-hour traffic headed to the suburbs. Agent Wagner suggested we meet at her office and hybrid images of CSI and Miami Vice immediately sprang to mind. I anticipated a law enforcement complex with unmarked Crown Victorias and muscled guys with short haircuts and shiny shoes. The destination contributed to my heightened scrutiny of the cars following me. I made the turns as prescribed and kept an eye on the road behind as the highways turned to off ramps and eventually a once vibrant commercial artery that now catered to Atlanta's growing Asian and Latino communities.

Halfway down the hill, behind the Red Roof Inn and between a repurposed Burger King and a small strip center anchored by a Western Union franchise, the entrance to an office park emerged. Executive Park had probably meant more to those leasing space in the 1970s, but the title seemed tired and dated to a contemporary audience. What had once been Class A space and host to big corporate names was now Class C space, and the current owners were thrilled by any lease terms and lengths. A government tenant was especially desirable; the reduction in rent was offset by the relative certainty that the monthly check would clear.

I drove through the maze of buildings, relieved that absolutely nobody was behind me, until I reached building 3240. There was no exterior signage other than the numbers, and the cars out front gave no indication that the upper floor of the building was leased to law enforcement. It wasn't until I had parked the car and walked through the empty lobby to the elevator that I was assured that I was even in the right place. The directory next to the elevator, once proudly listing IBM and other giants in shiny new letters, now listed among its residents simply GBI, Suite 302, in crooked letters against a faded background. I was simultaneously appalled at the depths being plumbed by our law enforcement agencies and thankful that the government was obviously spending as little as possible to house these folks.

I rode the elevator to the 3rd floor alone and couldn't help but wonder how the building's other occupants felt about their neighbors. Do they feel safer or targeted? Did they, at some point, stop looking over their shoulders as they walked through the parking lot as I had done and would repeat on the way out? The doors opened and I stepped out into a dismal hallway furnished with stained carpet and plastic ficus trees. Without the assortment of keypads and card swipes that adorned the door to the left, I might have wandered the halls looking for Suite 302. I approached the door, rang the doorbell on the keypad, and looked up to smile for a small camera in a corner above the door. A minute or so passed and I was reaching for the button again when a loud, steely click sounded and the door opened, pushed by agent Wagner holding a phone to her ear and apparently finishing a call. She waved me in.

"I'm aware of that, lieutenant," she said to the phone, "but I'm working to connect the subject to the premises before he gets capped, which seems likely."

I looked at her wide-eyed but, catching my expression, she shook her head and pointed at me, I assume to reassure me. I followed her through what appeared to be a random assemblage of used office furniture atop fraying and threadbare gray commercial carpet. Cubicles were partially assembled or disassembled and there was a yard-sale-feel to the space; no pictures on the walls, and desks without chairs and offices with only a phone on the floor. She walked through the barren maze and I followed close behind until she paused at a doorway and pointed into the room. I took a seat at the table as she finished the call.

"Sorry about that. He's on my ass about a different case. Not yours." She said all this without sitting.

"I have a case?" She almost smiled.

"You are party to an ongoing investigation," she said, stepping back out of the door and returning from the room next door to finish the sentence, "but you are not the subject of that investigation." She pulled a single sheet of paper from the file she had retrieved and placed it on the desk in front of me. "This is the administrative subpoena. You need to hold on to this."

"Okay. Should I read it?"

"Yes. It requires your assistance in evidence collection regarding the people listed there," she continued, pointing to a short list of names, one of which was Thib's. This made it official.

"I thought you said he wasn't in trouble."

"I never said that," she replied, sitting in the chair to my right. "I said he would have some choices to make, just as you do. Only he has had actual involvement."

"But you expect me to testify against him?"

"Thib? No. He's not the one we're after. Jeremiah, probably not, even though he is the one where after.

There are other factors that would probably preclude you from testifying."

"Because I'm Thib's brother?"

"Not really, but we'll get to that in a minute."

Another agent seemed to appear from nowhere and take a seat to my left. He didn't introduce himself but agent Wagner seemed to have expected it, and I wondered if it was standard choreography. As he began to ask questions, she stood and walked out.

"Mr. Felder," he said, "My name is Coates. How long have you known of your brother's involvement with our subject?"

"Do you mean Jeremiah?" He nodded. "A month, maybe. It has all gone by very fast."

"When you say all, what do you mean?"

"Just the strange things with Thib and this guy. It's been tough to keep it all straight. And now this part with my wife in the hospital. It's just been a hectic couple of weeks." Agent Wagner heard the last part returning to the room.

"Who's in the hospital?" She asked, taking her seat and placing a manila folder on the table in front of her.

"Molly."

"Everything okay?" She asked, looking past me to Agent Coates.

"Not really, but we'll work through it, I guess."

"Is it related to the samples you found," she continued, "because you said earlier that Thib had connected some things."

"That's part of it," I replied, looking between the two of them and not wanting to say anything more. They sensed my hesitation.

"Just so you know," Agent Coates said, "you are unlikely to tell us anything we don't already know. So you can't get anyone in trouble any deeper than they already are." He paused for effect, or at least it felt like he did. "Unless, of course, you withhold information. That makes it messy for you."

"That figures," I said. "He's been making a mess of my life for years." I shook my head and looked back at Agent Wagner. "He said he had given Molly a couple of samples, and maybe that's where it came from. Originally. But she's got more than a couple of samples, and apparently it's been a bigger issue than I thought."

"What makes you say that?"

"The doctor says the lab's still trying to make sense of her blood chemistry."

"Oh. And the baby?"

"All seems right in that world, according to the doctor. That's a conversation we haven't had yet." Agent Wagner nodded and looked past me to Coates before pulling a set of pictures from the folder and placing them in front of me on the table.

"Mugshots?" I asked.

"Just a formality," she replied. "Making sure we're talking about the same people." The first sheet had four pictures, one of which was Thib. I pointed him out.

"Know any of the others?"

"Nope. Should I?"

"Not necessarily. Just asking. How about these?" She asked, flipping to the next set of pictures.

"Jeremiah," I said, pointing to the face at the bottom on the left.

"And?"

"I don't remember faces on the others, but they could be the guys who kicked the stall in at my office. I mostly saw them behind the tinted windows and sunglasses."

"Just point out the ones you know for sure."

"He's the only one."

Next was another set of four black males and, after that, a sheet of four white males. When I didn't point out any of those, Agent Wagner flipped to a sheet of four white females. I looked at her with a confused expression but couldn't identify any of the faces. She flipped the sheet and again I scanned four more white female faces. The lower right picture stopped me cold. The picture was grainy, but Molly's face was clearly discernible.

"Why is Molly in these pictures?" I asked.

"Do you recognize any of the others?" Coates asked me. "Are they friends of your wife's? From work? Any look familiar?"

"No," I replied, slipping sheets back and forth, "but what has she got to do with any of this, and who are the others?" He looked past me to Agent Wagner. She pulled the next set of pictures. These were not mugshots but more like clips taken from video. It was difficult to see the faces, but the people in the pictures were naked and engaged in various sexual positions. I looked closely and recognized the face as one of the women in the previous pictures.

"Porn? Are you saying these women are in the porn business, and that Molly was somehow involved?"

"Not exactly," she said, flipping to the next page, another set of images with a different woman and a variety of males in different settings. I scanned the images and looked back at her with a question. She flipped to the next page. Same types of images, women with various men, naked, engaged in sexual positions. This time the face was clearly Molly's. I took a deep breath and closed my eyes, waiting for another deep breath before asking for clarity.

"Okay, this is obviously a lot bigger than I thought it was, so can you tell me what the hell is going on?"

"Paragraph 3 of your subpoena," Coates interjected, "stipulates that if you reveal any information to anyone outside this facility that compromises our investigation, such action will result in you being held criminally liable and subject to prosecution."

"So this doesn't leave the room," Agent Wagner continued.

"Okay," I surrendered, "whatever. Just tell me what's going on."

"The man you've identified as Thib," Wagner began, looking between Coates and me, "has emerged as a part of a separate investigation."

"You mean Thib's connected to more than one investigation?"

"Yes. And the second of these involves the distribution of stolen prescription narcotics."

"But not Jeremiah."

"Correct," she replied, with a nod to Coates. "This guy has been linked to several of the production lot numbers reported stolen, including the ones you gave me. At first I didn't see a connection. Then I remembered all the DNA research Thib was talking about and the lawyer that was helping him in exchange for computer work."

"So this lawyer's involved?"

"More than involved, it seems."

"And Thib is the connection to Molly?"

"Potentially," she continued. "The target market for these substances, at least for him, has been suburban women who enjoy a certain amount of free time but suffer from relationship or marital woes or dissatisfaction. Whatever the reason, the women are vulnerable and see the narcotics as a way of easing the pain of reality with a sharper edge and less visibility than alcohol."

"What the hell are you talking about?" I asked. "When you say vulnerable, do you mean Molly is a victim? Am I supposed to feel guilty because I drove her to drugs?"

"I'm just giving you the profile," Wagner replied. "I'm not pointing any fingers."

"Okay."

"The drugs are addictive," she continued, "like heroin or meth, and the addiction leads to a dependence on the source. If the women are already unhappy in their marriages, the access to the drugs seems to fuel something like moral turpitude, lowering the barriers of abnormal behavior and presenting them with what they perceive to be an escape hatch. Meanwhile, the lawyer, who primarily handles divorces and paternity cases, enjoys a steady stream of candidates."

"So how is Thib involved? My understanding was that he only did the guy's computer work."

Wagner pointed down to the photos on the table.

"So what are these images?"

"These videos were recovered from a hard drive we found in Thib's storage unit. The drive appears to contain a data dump from a computer in the lawyer's office, though it does not appear that the videos were recorded there. It does appear likely that these videos were intended to serve as leverage of some sort, keeping the dependence intact and the narcotics flowing."

"So it's like prostitution?"

"At this point, doubtful, at least in the normal sense. More like human trafficking or sex slavery, but we are not building a case against the women. Not at this point."

"But this will all be public?"

"Public record, yes," she replied, "though given the nature of the case, the judge may seal everything. We'll know more about that down the road. We will continue to be vigilant, but the media will have access at some point, whether or not they choose to do anything with this portion."

I could only stare at Agent Wagner with eyes squinted as her words flowed over me. I couldn't look at the images and I couldn't quite imagine what sort of title wave their release on the Internet might create. Somewhere in the porn universe a fetish existed for images like these and the video content from which they sprang. Porn. A woman whose sexual appetite I would've described as tepid at best making the rounds on the fetish circuit and she'd probably never know it. At least if she was lucky. But things did not appear to be going her way. It appeared to be proceeding more like a death spiral, possibly from a couple of samples.

"And you guys have been on this for a while?" I asked Wagner before turning to Coates, "following this story as it unfolded?"

"This part we suspected," Coates replied with a gesture back to the images, "mainly because it fits the profile. But we didn't uncover these until yesterday, and we're still processing a lot of it. We should be able to explain more when that part is behind us."

"And how much of this did Thib know about or have a part in?" I asked, turning back to Wagner. "Or can you tell me? Do I even want to know?"

"Can't say for sure at this point," Wagner continued, "but it seems likely that Thib's computer skills were instrumental in this guy's operation. From what we can tell, mainly from drilling down into the data on the hard drive and from my conversations with him over the last several months, Thib was installing security cameras and digital recorders as a part of the lawyer's unofficial surveillance offerings, work I considered legitimate until these other pieces came into view."

"And that's where he got the samples?"

"That seems to be the connection you've been looking for, yes."

"And he knew that Molly was involved in this?" I said, pointing back down to the images.

"It seems likely since he was involved in the installation of equipment and obviously had access to finished video. But, we can't say for sure at this point. I haven't seen anything yet that confirms that he knew anything about Molly's direct involvement."

"Or his direct involvement, since he doesn't appear in any of the videos either, correct?"

"Correct. At least the film we've seen so far. As I said, we are still processing it and we should know more when we complete that step."

"So he may have just been the AV guy, installing the cameras and capturing the surveillance footage, without any connection to the drugs, beyond what he said about the initial samples."

"Well, it may have gone a little beyond that," she said, glancing at Coates and softly clearing her throat. "If that were true, why would he keep a copy of all the data in his storage unit? He knew something was going on."

Much Later That Evening

Molly's breathing was steady and her eyes were closed. The digital clock on the wall behind her bed read 11:17, the passing of time marked by nurses taking vital signs every couple of hours and the soundless reflection of light from the television. Her saline IV had a smaller cocktail plug into the line, but I had missed the doctor's visit earlier that evening and would have to wait until the next morning for an explanation. The net effect was largely one of sedation, though every once in a while Molly's brows would furrow and her lips would move as if she were asking someone a difficult question. Then her face would relax as if the answer had been satisfactory.

This particular hall of this particular floor had proven to be very quiet. I walked up and down the polished floors framed by partially closed doors as nurses wheeled diagnostic pods and computer stands from room to room. At some point we stopped nodding to each other as we passed, recognizing that our time together was set, our relationship prescribed at least until the next shift change. And we danced our nocturnal ballet until sometime after midnight, when the hallway tickled my claustrophobia and I set out in search of new tile to traverse. And vending.

Down a short hallway just off the main cafeteria, I stumbled onto the chapel, its doorway framed in dark wood with a small sign to the right of the casement declaring that the chapel was open to all. I opened the door and stepped inside, letting the door close quietly behind me. The lights appeared to be triggered by a switch in the doorframe, as a couple of the corner bulbs were struggling under the sudden surge, casting a disco effect on the edges of the small altar at the front. The room appeared to have been carved out of two treatment rooms, and the crucifix hung at the center of the space between two heavily-draped windows. Beneath the cross was a kneeler framed by two short rows of wooden pews. A minimalist, almost spartan feel enveloped the space. There were no pictures on the walls and the lighting, now in full bloom, offered little competition for the darkness, except for spots like the cross and the kneeler. I took a seat two rows from the front and tried to remember the last time I'd sat in a pew.

Looking at the pool of light and the cross within, I was struck by an idea. One might expect such a revelation to have been divine, but that supposition loses traction when I reveal the idea, specifically that the gift shop for Evangeland should be designed like a cross, just as many Christian churches are. An aerial photograph of the park would eventually include a prominent cross as a part of the layout. I kept leaning my head left and right and mapping that image on the site plan I had in my mind, and I didn't notice that someone else had entered the chapel until I heard the almost silent click of the door closing. I looked back as a young man in green scrubs took a seat in the back pew. I sat for another minute or so and then stood and walked back toward the door.

"I hope I didn't mess you up," the man said.

"Not at all," I replied. "I feel the same way. I'm not looking to distract you while you're here. You're probably pretty busy about now."

"Not distracting me," he replied with a shrug. "I'm not much of a church person."

"No?"

"Nope," he said, "so you go ahead with what you are doing. Don't worry about me."

"Why here," I said, looking around, "if you're not much of a church person? If you don't mind me asking?"

"Don't mind at all. It's all about quiet."

"Even on a night shift? I would've thought this time of day would be quiet."

"It is quieter than a hectic day shift, but the workflow is the same. I come in here mostly to unplug from it all for five or ten minutes, like a smoke break without the cancer."

"Good way to look at it."

"Thanks. How about you? What brings you?"

"Boredom, mostly. My wife is in a room upstairs and I needed new floor tiles to count."

"Well, I hope you found some peace in this quiet," he said with a nod.

"Unfortunately, I'm not much of a church person either, but you are right about quiet."

"Why's that unfortunate?"

"I don't know," I replied, raising an eyebrow and pointing to the cross at the front. "I guess in this setting it seems like it would be a whole lot easier. Just let go and let God."

"Sounds like you doubt your doubt."

"Not really. Just work-related."

"What kind of work do you do?"

"Develop real estate." His brow furloughed as he tried to make the connections. "Here's a question for you," I continued, "and then I'll leave you alone. From a healthcare provider's perspective, and one who's not a church person, how do you feel when recovery is answered prayer and death is failed science?"

"I don't really have those conversations as a rule. Most of my patients, and their families, are religious, mostly because of geography I would guess. And they pray a lot and really do find peace in that quiet. So who am I to rock that boat? You know? Whatever gets you through the night."

"Good way to look at that, too," I said, reaching for the door. "Thanks."

"Bread and circus, though, if you really think about it. I mean, just because it gets you through the night doesn't make it true."

"What do you mean?"

"Well, it's all a fiction, really. A human construct given divine characters. We've invented religions through the slow march of time to control the masses, to feed and entertain them so nobody asks too many questions and powered establishments are maintained."

"Damn, you've given this some thought."

"Not in a long while," he replied. "I developed a quick response after being asked a million times why I didn't go to church. After hearing that, most folks just smile and nod and walk away."

"I would imagine so. I should be going."

"See what I mean? But you asked," he said with a chuckle.

"Yes, I did."

"Besides, if you think about it at all, with any level of objectivity, it stops making sense pretty quickly. Some of the stories are fascinating, though, and you can tell why they would be interesting to kids, and maybe even adults who didn't want to think too much."

"You got a favorite story?"

"Not really, but the Jonah story comes to mind."

"You want to live in a whale?"

"Not a whale," he said with a smile. "It was a big fish. That's an important distinction to some. I've never figured out why that's an important narrative, but it's a hell of a visual image."

"How would you incorporate that story and image into a theme park?"

"What do you mean?" He asked. "Why would I do something like that?"

"That's the project I'm working on right now. A Bible experience theme park."

"Wow. How's that working out for you?"

"Pays the bills the same way a retail site does, I suppose. It's new to me, but it's been an interesting challenge." I reached again and opened the door before turning back to him. "Enjoyed your perspective. Thanks."

"Me, too. Good luck. Hope the best for your wife, too."

"Thanks," I said, closing the door behind me and stepping into the hall. Turning left down the hall I passed the dark cafeteria on the way to the main lobby and the parking deck beyond. Molly was sleeping and I determined my best strategy was to do the same.

September 10

It was 9:15 the next morning as I retraced my steps from the parking deck to the main lobby of the hospital. The intervening seven hours brought me little sleep, and only the shower and change of clothes seemed to separate me from the day before. The lobby television caught my eye as I walked through. The local network news was breaking the story about Jeremiah, the first of many times his face would be on the television screen. I paused to catch the last half of the story, including his attorney's assurance that Jeremiah was innocent and that the charges were just another example of the atheist secular state imposing its will on good Christian people and throwing the whole country into moral relativism and blatant disregard for God's laws. I muttered that a good fallback position might be a first amendment reference to his freedom of religious expression, anticipating that a real court might want some connection to actual human law.

"I don't think it'll get that far," a familiar voice said from behind me. I turned to look at Thib before turning back to the close of the news segment.

"What makes you so sure?" I asked after the story was over.

"Can't be sure, but my lawyer says it's unlikely to make it to a jury."

"You have a lawyer?"

"Yep. Same guy I was telling you about. The one who does all the paternity testing."

"You're not likely to face a judge in Family Court, Thib. This is pretty serious shit, way beyond custody and child support."

"Let me worry about that. Besides, speaking of child support, you didn't tell me Molly was pregnant."

"I didn't officially know until last night, and Molly I haven't really had a chance to talk about it."

"Yeah. That's what she said a minute ago. I went up for a visit. She looks great, though. Glowing, I think is what I'm supposed to say. So, congratulations. I'm going to be an uncle."

I didn't know how to respond, so I just looked through him to the receptionist desk and the volunteers helping eager faces find loved ones in the system and the building. Several people had stepped in to occupy seats in the lobby waiting area and a maintenance worker was mopping up a spill in front of the small coffee shop. And then Thib was talking again.

"Chad, man, are you surprised, or what? Dude, you look shocked. You okay? No wonder you were riding my ass on the phone last night. You've got a baby in the mix now. That changes everything."

"I was riding your ass because you fucked up again and dragged me and my family into it."

"Whatever. Dude, you have to move past all this. You're going to be a Dad. What a shocker!"

"More than you know."

"What's that supposed to mean?" He asked.

"It means that it's time for me to check on my wife," I replied. "Thanks for stopping in to check on her. I'll let you know what the doctor says. Good luck with all that," I said, pointing to the television before turning and walking down the hall to the elevator.

The stainless steel doors opened at the nurses' station. The faces had changed with the arrival of the day shift in the hallways were abuzz with nurses and equipment. When I opened the door to Molly's room, she was awake and her nurse was finishing up her inventory of vital signs. Molly gave me the tired smile and sad eyes of a woman beleaguered by the machinations of detox and the uncertainty of pregnancy.

"How are we doing this morning?" I asked of everyone in the room. The nurse produced the first answer.

"We are doing much better this morning," she replied cheerfully, wrapping the blood pressure gauge armband around the monitor on her rolling diagnostic stand. "Vitals are strong and I think the doctor will be by shortly. He's just down the hall. Is there anything I can get you in the meantime?" she asked, smiling to Molly, who just shook her head in response. With a smile and a nod, the nurse left. I sat on the edge of the bed.

"You're looking a little more chipper this morning. You get a good nights sleep?"

"I did," she replied quietly. "I don't think I've had this much sleep in a while."

"Sleep is a good thing," I replied with a smile.

"Tears can be too, but I don't think I have any left. I have really made a mess of things."

"Life is messy," I replied calmly, "but we'll get it figured out."

"I'm not sure where to begin."

"Well, the good news is I can probably let you off the hook for explaining most of it. Others did a lot of that for you while you were sleeping, at least the part about the drugs."

"I don't understand," she replied. "Are you talking about the doctors and the lab results?"

"No, I haven't heard those results, yet. But I have a better idea of what those results will be based on last night's discussion with the GBI."

"Oh. What did they say about me?"

"They mostly let the pictures tell the story."

"Pictures? What pictures?" Her eyes widened.

"Some of your activity was recorded." She closed her eyes and a tear slipped out as she shook her head. "Apparently," I continued, "your source was building leverage with all the women involved. Probably the men, too."

Molly took a deep breath as a tear slipped out the side of both eyes. "I'm so sorry," she whispered, "so sorry."

"Like I said, we'll get it figured out."

"I don't know how," she replied. "And, at this point, I don't even know why."

There was a knock on the door and it opened as the doctor from the previous day walked in. He wore a tie and a white lab coat with a stethoscope sticking out of the pocket. He seemed to review the file as he walked in, checking for lab results and names.

"Well, how are we this morning?" He asked almost rhetorically before moving to the next question. "Anything new to report since yesterday?"

"Only that it's probably a little more complicated than originally thought," I said, shooting a comforting grin at Molly, "but we'll get it figured out." Her half smile response was less than convincing.

"Well," the doctor replied, "life has a way of getting complicated, but we are here to simplify it if we can." He set the file on the table at the foot of the bed and pulled the small armchair close to the bed and sat facing the two of us.

"Toxicology came back," he began, "and shows a mixture of prescription drugs that should never have crossed. The details of that are not as relevant as the steps we take from this point forward. We started you on methadone, and that will mitigate some of the initial discomfort of detox, but the levels and combinations in your bloodstream are toxic. Our goal will be to stabilize that in the right direction while we set up a recovery program to get you back up and running. Here's what I need you to hear: all we can do is all we can do. In the end, you have to throw the monkey off your back. Husbands, doctors, and twelve-step programs are here to support you, but you have to do the heavy lifting, and it will be heavy. Some of the substances in your system are among the most addictive known. But people do it every day, and you can too. And at this point you have the ultimate incentive growing inside of you. And that's as simple as I can make it. I'm going to let that settle in a bit and I'll be back to answer questions a little later this morning, unless you have any questions at this point?"

Molly closed her eyes but didn't respond.

"Thanks," I replied. "I think we'll have some for you when you come back."

The doctor left. The ambient noise from the hallway faded behind the closing door, and the silence in Molly's room was crushing. Her eyes remained closed and our conversation seemed to pause, so I got up from the edge of the bed and walked to the window. The sky was blue and the sun was bright as I looked out over a short section of flat roof to the lot beyond where a new wing of the hospital was under construction, groups of men and women raising a structure where there was none before, building something together that is potentially a force for good. People build lives the same way, I thought, watching the intricate choreography. I've been around enough construction sites to know that there was a method to the madness. But what would happen if the building, almost complete, just collapsed upon itself, maybe even injuring or killing people in the process? Where did the workers muster the strength to build again? And what if, like Ayn Rand's Howard Roark, one of the crew thought collaboration to be overrated and brought about the destruction purposefully. How does a culture establish ownership of a building, or a life?

In the distance, beyond the construction, a steeple rose among the pines, cross perched atop a shuttered belfry. There was the strength for many, but not for all. And given that strength, and the human frailty that seemed to draw it from ancient texts, where did free will come into play? Framed by the construction, I was reminded of work and the challenge of animating the concept of free will. Somehow that idea remained way too abstract in my mind to be mixed with dinosaurs in the Garden of Eden or an ark with a garden in the bilge. And where had free will been in Molly's world? To assume her choices allowed her to be victimized by evil required an active Satan, and that requires an all-knowing and all-powerful deity, a personal God with hands on all the buttons and switches. Why would such a God allow His creation to be dragged into dependence and slavery, even if the initial mistake was hers, if He could do something about it? And why would He bring a child into all that?

"I'm so sorry," Molly said softly, "for all of this. Nobody would blame you if you just turned and walked away. I am a train wreck."

"People always like to watch a train wreck," I replied. "They can't turn away. But," I continued, walking back to the edge of the bed, "we'll get this figured out and the tracks cleared and the trains running again."

"I'm sorry I didn't tell you about the baby. I hate that you had to find out the way you did. Not the best way to find out that you're going to be a Dad. I should've told you sooner."

"Well, there are things I should've told you too, but let's not worry about all that right now. Let's just focus on getting you up and running again. Nothing else really matters at this point."

By the end of the third night in the hospital, Molly had wrestled some real demons. Her face filled and flushed with the continued IV, but even in her sleep she seemed to squeeze every ounce of blood from her brow and cheeks. A look of intense anguish would suddenly grip her face and then would just as abruptly leave as neurons fired and synapses filled, trying to accommodate a new chemistry. Nurses and doctors came and went. Social services caseworkers interviewed and documented the changing conditions of mother and child with a strange but clinical interest, much the same as afforded crack babies and heroin babies. Their perspective, I assumed, was that addiction was addiction, and it never mixed well with pregnancy, a humbling socio-cultural reality for those of us who thought we'd transcended such human weaknesses.

No matter how many times and how fervently my eyes affirmed that I had nothing to do with all this, my inclusion in the family's escape plan from addiction suggested guilt by association, and maybe I carried more guilt than I thought. Agent Wagner's profile description of those women in the images included rocky marriages, separate lives, histories of infidelity and disposable income. The money was not as much a price for the drugs as the cost of admission to the target market. I owned part of that history.

While we were in the hospital beginning our escape from addiction, I didn't ask Molly for any of the details. At the suggestion of the caseworker, we looked only to the future. There would be time down the road, she assured us, to work through the issues that led to our addiction. By the end of the third day I understood the strategy surrounding the collective pronouns. Even if I'd had nothing to do with the drugs, as my eyes kept saying, the path forward required all stakeholders to grab the torch to break the darkness. Light the path or get the hell out of the way, the eyes looking back at me continued to say, but don't fool yourself into thinking you didn't play a role here. The fact that I was still there after three days only strengthened their resolve. Too many, I assumed, cut and run. Some with very good reasons, arguments available to me that, at least to this point, had gone unused. At the end of the third day, I silently renewed our marriage vows, especially the sickness and health part.

The greatest test, perhaps, came early after our homecoming. Within the first week of her discharge, Molly needed to find a recovery group and begin the assimilation process. I had worked with such groups as a seminarian and as a young pastor, but my involvement was mainly setting aside a physical space for weekly meetings, making sure the coffee pots worked, and being available if someone wanted spiritual counseling. Recovery groups are largely pantheistic, focusing on a power larger than self. So I was never really called on to espouse a particular theology. The goal was sobriety, not conversion, and a particular religious tradition enabled an addict to neglect the hard work, to let go and let God, and such a release was not part of the recovery process.

There was, though, a fervor in their association, the frenetic caffeine consumption and chain-smoking, that joined with their efforts at anonymity to achieve a cult-like stature in my limited perspective. The participants seemed almost addicted to the recovery process, and I've had relationships with drunks that I preferred to single conversations with guys in recovery. They could be insufferable zealots in the presence, or with even the mention, of alcohol. But that had always been them. Now it was us.

About a week or so after the first recovery meeting, the dust began to settle and the routine began to reestablish itself. Molly was talking about work again, though she was waiting for the right time to actually go back to the office. While her colleagues had not known the full details surrounding her leave of absence, there was probably a sense that it was more than just a much needed vacation. She was progressing as planned, struggling with fewer and fewer bouts of anxiety and desperation and leaning pretty heavily on the coffee, but the clouds seem to have lifted and she would leave the house and make the short but public trip to Starbucks. The anonymity and the flow of human traffic through the coffee shop seemed almost therapeutic, and she would share with me her speculations about the baggage all the other coffee drinkers probably carried. I can only assume it was helping her work through it.

September 19

Molly's emerging confidence and independence sent me back to the office and the projects lurking there. New strip centers seemed to spring up almost weekly. I partnered with a group to explore an industrial manufacturing complex near the interstate and the MARTA line, potentially mixed-use with lofts above restaurant and retail. I was back in the flow and every day the mail brought a new surprise.

That Tuesday was no different. Among the invoices and bank statements and credit card offers that comprised the mail that day was a plain envelope with no return address. My name and address on the front was printed and I was reminded of how computers were eliminating the wonder of cursive. I opened the envelope and found a single sheet of paper, a message written in the same block print as the address. The hair on the back of my neck immediately stood up as I read the note.

"Fear not the jackal, known or unknown. I have seen him and he is us. He waits on the other side."

The note was obviously from Thib. I hadn't spoken to him since our passing in the hospital lobby, but the cryptic jackal reference could only come from him. I had no idea what he was talking about but it didn't sound good. I called his cell phone but after two rings got the recorded announcement that the number was no longer in service. Stumped by the question of who to call next who might know how to find him, I pulled out my wallet and fished out the card Agent Wagner had given me along with the subpoena. I called the cell number listed on the card and she answered after two rings.

"Wagner," she said

"Hey," I replied. "This is Chad. You got a second?"

"As long as you're not calling from my bedroom closet."

"We're safe there," I replied. "I think I'm past that phase of my mid-life crisis."

"Moved on to Porsches, I guess."

"Not exactly, but I am looking for Thib. His cell phone is no longer in service and I didn't know if you'd had any reason to see him."

"Saw him last week," she replied. "He came in so we could begin sweeping up the details. We talked for a while, looked through some pictures, established some connections."

"How bad is it?"

"I pulled him aside at the end and suggested he get a good lawyer, but my hunch is a plea deal will keep him out of the fire. He's not the target."

"But you haven't heard from him since?"

"No. Why do you ask?"

"I got a strange note in the mail today, one only he could write and it's got a tone to it."

"A tone? Read it to me."

"Yeah. Fear not the jackal, known or unknown. I have seen him and he is us. He waits on the other side."

"Who is the jackal?"

"It's a reference to the suicide note my mother left. I kept it from him for a long time, but he somehow dug it out of my closet."

"Was that why he went to Vegas and then did all that DNA testing?"

"Had something to do with that, I think. From the suicide note he seemed to conclude that the Jumper was the jackal."

"Who now is him, and he waits on the other side."

"Yep."

"What's your next move?"

"The storage unit."

"I'll meet you there."

I pulled into the storage complex about 20 minutes later. A black Crown Victoria with tinted windows was the only other car in the lot. As I parked a couple of spaces away, Wagner got out of the Crown Vic and we walked together to the automatic doors in the elevator beyond. We didn't say anything, even as we got off the elevator and worked our way through the maze of metal doors and motion-activated fluorescent lights to Thib's unit.

"Thib," I said loudly, knocking on metal door, "you in there?" I looked at the latch. There was no lock, and no answer. I reached for the handle of the bottom of the door and pulled the door up and open.

As the light filled space, all the boxes and clutter looked the same, surrounding the bed and the apparently lifeless body of Thibodeaux Felder. Having had my morbid assumption affirmed, I could only stand and shake my head. Wagner moved purposefully into the unit and to the bed to check for a pulse. I watched as she placed three fingers across his neck. Then she stopped. She didn't feel the need to turn around and confirm anything. Instead, she pulled a pen from her pocket and stuck it into the neck of a small plastic pill bottle on the bed next to his right hand. She examined the bottle and then replaced it and walked back to the door.

"I'm sorry for your loss," she said, then moved into the main hallway and made a call before returning to the open doorway. "I take it you suspected we'd find something like this?"

"I guess I did," I replied, "but I sure hoped we wouldn't. Not like this, anyway. What was in the bottle?"

"Valium. And even that is odd. With the variety of new and very effective options out there for this maneuver, and he had clear access to all of them, he went really old school with the Valium."

"That makes sense."

"How's that?"

"That was our mother's drug of choice. Killed herself the same way."

"Well, there's a certain symmetry to that, I guess."

This doesn't even make sense," I said after a pause, trying to reconcile the series of events that might've led to this. "You said he wasn't even the target, so why this?"

"He wasn't our target, and remember, Chad, I told you he'd have some choices to make?"

"Yes, but I didn't think this was one of them. I mean, shit. Was he in this deep?"

"With us he was looking at a plea deal, but he was going to have to connect a lot of dots and testify to stay out of prison. That was the primary choice he was looking at."

"There has to have been a better way out."

"If there was, it doesn't look like he found it. I know he's dead and he's your brother and all, but try not to back up and make him out to be an innocent victim here, even in your own mind. This is no prodigal son story."

I didn't know how to respond.

"He made choices all along the way. We all do. Some make better choices, that's all." She paused. The highway sounds crept in to fill the silence. "And some of his were really bad."

"What's that supposed to mean?" I said, looking at her for an explanation. "After all, he was still my brother. He was a good kid. Always meant well. Had a big heart. And now he was dead. No need to keep kicking him."

"He shows up in the videos," she said facing Thib before turning to face me, "with Molly."

The revelation stunned me and I held her gaze until her cell phone rang and she turned to walk down the hall and take the call. I turned back to face my dead brother and the relative shambles his life had fallen into. Boxes stacked on boxes, full of photo albums and other artifacts of our family's existence. Clothes spilling out of duffle bags and hanging from the wire mesh ceiling, probably left to dry after being washed in the bathroom sink of the main floor lobby. This was the dark side of family.

Wagner had not returned by the time the motion sensors killed the lights above the unit, so I stepped up on the small plastic stool next to the bed and clapped the lights back on. Stepping down, I noticed the Nietzsche on the stack of boxes next to the bed. Instinctively, I pulled the book from the box and fanned through it, half expecting Thib's voice to rise from the pages. Instead, he spoke from the inside front cover. There, in the same block lettering, Thib had recorded what I could only assume to be some final thoughts.

"The mistakes are mine and there have been many. I own them and I owe them. They have defined my path and determined my interaction with the physical world. For me, there is nothing more and nothing less. Holy shit, what a ride."

Later That Evening

The house smelled of garlic and blue cheese, and the sounds coming from the kitchen suggested that Molly had been cooking. It had always been just the two of us, so cooking had never really been a priority. Molly must have sensed my amusement by the curious expression on my face.

"I figured I better start learning how to cook," she said, walking toward me and rubbing her belly. Her eyes were smiling but betrayed an afternoon of tears. She wrapped her arms around me in a tentative hug.

"I'm so sorry about Thib," she said into my shoulder. "I don't know what else to say."

"Been a long day," I replied, matching her arm for arm.

"You doing okay?" She asked.

"Just getting older by the minute."

"I'd fix you a stiff drink if I could," she continued, "but we got rid of all the good stuff."

"Not sure it would really help much at this point," I replied, remembering that we'd cleared the house of drugs and alcohol as part of the recovery process. "No need to slow the processing of all this stuff at this point."

"Do you feel like talking? There are things you should know if you're trying to figure all this out." Her arms loosened their grip, but her cheek didn't want to leave my shoulder to reveal a past I was already trying to reconcile.

"Let's leave that for another day," I replied, reaffirming our bond with a tightened hug. "I think I just left a lot of that stuff in storage, and time will tell if we ever really need to unpack it."

"Are you sure?"

"Very sure. Like the therapist keeps saying, move the ball forward. Besides, I'm hungry. Let's focus on what you got cooking."

Dinner was quiet, comfortable food and conversation. After rinsing dishes and loading the dishwasher, Molly and I settled in for hot tea and television. Our situation had prompted us to reclaim the den as well as the kitchen, and the domesticity of it all was palpable. We'd sat on the sofa more in the last several weeks than we had in the entire time we'd owned it. Molly's exercise regimen had changed, and she no longer went to the gym during the evening. Nights were beginning to look a lot like this one, though the selection of TV shows was usually better.

"I'm going to take a shower," I told Molly, handing her the remote. "Maybe something good will be on by the time I come back down."

She looked up from her pregnancy book and smiled. Molly had achieved a new calm and she smiled more often. Sometimes they look forced, but not this time. She seemed genuinely happy, settling into her new role and exploring the expectations. Calm was emerging as the new happy in our world.

Getting undressed, I fished everything out of my pockets, including the letter from Thib. I opened it up and read it again, shaking my head in wonder. After neatly folding the letter back into the envelope, I reached up to the top shelf of my closet and pulled down the small box labeled seminary, the same one I'd rummaged through a month or so earlier. I set the box on the plastic stool I'd used to reach it and opened it. I pulled out the Bible my father had given me and opened it to insert Thib's note. It seemed like an appropriate spot to hold references to jackals.

The book fell open to a familiar spot and tucked inside was my mother's original suicide note, mysteriously returned to its resting place for more than 20 years. I opened it and read it as well, shaking my head in wonder. Looking back at the Bible, I noticed that all three of the colorful bookmark threads had been positioned to hold that page as well. It was the story of Cain and Abel, the only sons of Adam and Eve and the bearers of original sin. Abel wins God's favor and Cain can't seem to get it together. Cain murders Abel and is exiled by God to a life of wandering. It is Cain's response to God's inquiry that the world has canonized, though I had long fought the idea that I was my brother's keeper. It had evolved into one of my smaller arguments with God, back when the arguments seemed important.

I put both notes back in the Bible and began to put it back in the box when a manila envelope caught my eye. The envelope was a new addition. I pulled it out of the box and opened it. First out of the envelope were three stacks of $100 bills, a lot of money for someone living on a ramen noodle diet in a storage unit. Next was a stack of papers. Most of these I recognized as the DNA research Thib had been conducting. The last two of the sheets looked like printouts of some type of online records.

At the top of the first, in the appropriate boxes, my name was listed along with my previous address and my doctor's name. This looked like an official record, a page from my medical file dated about ten years earlier. It even had my signature at the bottom. In the box titled "procedure," only one word was written: vasectomy. Apparently Thib had hacked into my medical records. The date stamp listed with the URL at the bottom of the page was the same day that we'd spoken in the hospital lobby, the same day he'd congratulated me on becoming a father.

The second sheet was dated several days after the first, and the name on the record was Molly Duncan Felder. It was the results of a DNA test using a procedure called SNP Microarray which, I would learn later, is a non-invasive procedure that tests the baby's DNA found naturally in the mother's bloodstream. The potheads in the lab coats had the game completely figured out. And so did Thib. The lab results connected his DNA with Molly's baby. All the while he'd had a hunch that his DNA was in play, a hunch given credibility when he visited Molly that morning, just before we passed in the lobby going in opposite directions. While there were no handwritten notes on the printout, it seemed clear that Thib wanted me to know that he knew. "I brought this child into the world," he might have written, but didn't, "so I'm going to take myself out." Even though the child was only a small part of the larger mess he'd made, his evocation of family symmetry was obvious and now complete.

At the bottom of the envelope was a small snapshot, the color fading and the edges worn. In the picture were two shirtless young boys on the tailgate of a truck. The older boy has his arm draped over the other's shoulder as he casts a confident smile for the camera. The younger wears a tentative smile and looks up at the older. There was no mischief in his eyes. I guess that would come later. There was only the search for affirmation, the validation that perhaps only an older brother could've offered. I guess I failed him on that one. Stuffing the picture back into the envelope with the evidence that Molly was carrying Thib's child, I realized that we had failed each other, Thib and I, that there was too much Cain in both of us and that the world wasn't as Edenic as either of us had hoped.

As I began repacking the box, I noticed another new addition. Thib had been busy on his final visit to my closet. In the space beneath where the envelope had been and under the original resting spot for what was essentially the Felder Family Bible and collection of suicide notes, I found a small, empty Coke bottle. I smiled through the tears.

With our parents dead and no family business or property binding us together, biology had become our only real connection. Even if life took brothers off the grid, it seemed DNA brought them back together. But how strong should biological bonds really be? To what extent was I expected to be my brother's keeper. The thought of raising another man's child, even Thib's, with a woman I was only beginning to get to know after four years of marriage seemed foreign to me, like it was happening to somebody else. As Dan Richards had said in Cincinnati, I had made my decisions about those things many years before. He had been talking about religion, and he had been correct, but he had chosen kids as his analogy. Even if I didn't want any, and I didn't, boots were going to hit the ground running. Boots with my brother's feet in them, and his genes. My family's genes. My genes.

And beyond biology, our other connection had been and was history, a family narrative rife with the tragedy of betrayal and the apparent inevitability of suicide, the kind of story that Darwinian evolution shouldn't favor. But the story was set to continue with or without a leading man, and Thib was using the cardboard box full of my past to make an aggressive argument for the shape of my future. Sitting on the floor of my closet holding the small bottle, I was listening as the essential words of Dan Richards and Evangeland poured from the bottle like the sound of the ocean from a shell. Love and hope, it whispered. It was all about love and hope.

I was creating an idealized experience of a deity I no longer valued because such an experience offered lots of people a feeling of unconditional love and eternal hope. We would design it, build it, and deliver it to the world, the brainchild of one, parented by many, for the benefit of people I'd grown to consider delusional. Downstairs, watching mindless television and rubbing her belly, was the woman who shared my bed and carried my dead brother's child. Soon to be flung into a very real world where we become the product of choices, that child was going to need love and hope. While I might've written it differently, my family story continued to unfold before me. I didn't need to be a Christian to understand that. Just human.

Three Years Later

The air was crisp, the sky was blue, and the parking lot was full. Such a combination might be considered the Holy Trinity among mainstream theme park operators, but Evangeland was neither mainstream nor interested in redefining any trinities, holy or otherwise. We walked through the lot to the main entrance and stepped inside the visitor center and up to the ticket counter. The friendly woman behind the counter greeted us warmly.

"Welcome to Evangeland, where the word of the Lord is your guide to fun and salvation. How old are you, young fella?" She asked, looking down at the child holding my hand.

"How old are you, Thibodeaux?" I asked, looking between his eyes and hers. He released my hand and held up three small fingers to indicate his age but didn't say anything. I used my newly released hand to fish my wallet out of my front pocket and Thibodeaux pulled tighter on his other arm and wrapped himself around Molly's leg. She reached down and picked him up and perched him on her hip.

"Thibodeaux," the ticket lady repeated, "now that's a great name. Is that a family name?" She asked.

"It was my brother's name," I replied, handing her a credit card.

"That's nice," she replied, swiping the card and printing the tickets. "It's nice to keep those family connections alive." She handed me the tickets and pointed toward the main lobby. "The Garden of Eden is that way and, as we all know, everything begins there! You are a good looking family, and I hope you have a blessed day."

"Thanks," I replied, pocketing my wallet and pointing our attractive family ship in the right direction. I had been to Evangeland a number of times, including two visits since it formally opened, but always as a consultant or a part of the design team. This was my first visit as a pure consumer and one suggested by Molly, whose recovery process had been successful in, among other things, rekindling an all but lost spirituality. While she expressed no attraction to the idea of an active and personal God, Molly's exercise regimen had grown to include meditative yoga and teaching a liberal strain of Christian Pilates at the ecumenical community church that leased the sanctuary and fellowship hall of the old Mountaintop Baptist campus. Word had it that the church had an option on the rest of the campus if they hit their growth targets and tithing goals. We attended no services or Bible studies and made no effort to join that or any other church, but Molly felt the expected responsibility to at least introduce her child, our child, to the world of God and organized religion. And so we made the pilgrimage up I-85 to Charlotte and now worked our way into the Garden of Eden, a large atrium space with animatronic Adam and Eve and a couple of dinosaurs, including one with a saddle.

"The saddle is an interesting touch," Molly said, as we eased through the crowd. "That your idea?"

"No," I said quickly. "That's a little too young earth for my taste."

At the rear of the garden, the lobby diverged and signage reflected a choice of Old or New Testament. As we had predicted in the design process, most visitors or patrons would choose the Old Testament, and that option had been built out as the most obvious. As we were cast out of the Garden with the others, the Old Testament world appeared before us. The Holy Moses Log Ride with the bulrushes and pyramid and elaborate Red Sea plumbing at the end. Thibodeaux was still too young for any of the rides, but he seemed captivated by them nonetheless as he watched from his large stroller. Molly, too, was wide-eyed as we walked underneath the traditional roller coaster, Heaven and Hell, that climbed high above us and ascended beneath us, the screams fading as the tracks disappeared into the dark, only to reemerge and climb to new heights.

"What's it like in Hell," she asked, pointing down into the tunnel.

"Probably a lot like detox," I replied, "scary stretch of anguish and uncertainty and then you come out at the other end, back into the light and happy to be there."

"Sounds about right," she replied with a blink.

Eventually we crossed into the New Testament, a sign at the entrance suggesting that a new covenant had been formed between God and His people. Sheep and lambs grazed pastorally beneath the sign as the entrance gave way to a small manger scene set on a stage surrounded by a landscaped seating area. A small sign at the entrance indicated that the next show would begin in 15 minutes, and a handful of people waited patiently for the birth of Jesus. As we passed the gift shop at the show's exit, Thibodeaux noticed the stuffed lambs and had to have one, especially when he discovered that when he pulled the bell on its collar a deep voice spoke a variety of Bible verses.

We approached the entrance to the Dark Night of the Soul, the centrifuge with the disappearing floor, and I could hear Wagner cranking up the Valkyries. Overcome with childhood curiosity, I gave in to the temptation and queued up with the faithful. Molly strolled Thibodeaux to the upper observation platform that offered a full view down into the cylinder. Once aboard, I looked up and spotted them among the anxious, smiling faces just as the Valkyries began their flight anew.

As a kid, my experience of the centrifuge had been rooted in the present. Was I going to fall beneath the receding floor and into the gears below, crushed to death by my own need for excitement? Now fully grown and lumbering through middle age, the Dark Night of the Soul was an amazingly prescient title. Cacophony reigned as the spinning wall pulled my back into the steel and the floor began to recede. I watched the faces around me in the cylinder, recognizing in the various stages of life represented there what, in my own life, could have been but was not to be. I was not going to go to law school or med school as some of the crowd had no doubt done, probably making their parents very proud at graduations and cocktail parties. The business world, while it had been a welcome diversion from my original clergy path, held no great promise for those not truly motivated by money. I was paying the bills and buying time, swapping hours for dollars without gaining ground on whatever my true passion was.

In that sense, the musical chaos was like an MRI, the picture of a mind scattered across disciplines, searching for fulfillment where there was none to be had, and that was the life I was prepared to see flash before my eyes as the cylinder continued to spin. I looked at the happy young families and realized that

I was never getting that phase of my life back, never going to escape the dysfunction that so clearly defined my own childhood and kept creeping back into my ongoing adulthood. The past had fallen beneath the floor, ground up by the gears and helicopter rotors and pill bottles. Here, pinned against the wall of the present looking at the others aging alongside me in the centrifuge, I sensed a peace come upon me as the noise was displaced by the soft rising of Amazing Grace from the integrated Dolby Sound System as the floor rose to embrace my feet again and I realized that, while I certainly owned them, I probably owed my own mistakes a debt of gratitude. As the ride slowed to a stop, I looked up and locked eyes with Thibodeaux. His father's words were never more true. Holy shit, what a ride.

Opposite the exit for The Dark Night of the Soul was a static display of the Last Supper, only this one had seats that patrons could occupy. We tried to get Thibodeaux out of the stroller for a picture, but the Lamb of God was still booming compelling verses. Just as we were about to re-enter the flow of traffic on the main sidewalk, a procession appeared, led by an actor cast as Jesus, arms outstretched on the cross beam, being led to Calvary by Roman soldiers. We followed behind until the procession, now numbering in the dozens, reached its destination and the players re-enacted the crucifixion as more than 300 watched in varying degrees of rapture from the small amphitheater's rows of benches.

"Why are those people crying," Thibodeaux asked as we were making our way out of the venue. "Are they sad?"

"They're sad," Molly replied, "because someone very special to them has died."

"Why?" he asked.

"Why are they sad or why did he die?"

"Why did he die?"

"He died to save us from our mistakes," she said, looking back at me near the end of the statement before looking back at him. "We all make mistakes because we are human. You'll make them too. We all do. But we will forgive you, and we will always love you."

"Horses!" Thibodeaux pointed from the stroller. Can we ride the horses? Please?"

Ahead was the final ride in the park, the Carousel of the Apocalypse. The carousel itself had been found in a retired amusement park in New Jersey and refurbished completely, including the replacement of all the previous animals with white horses. Everybody rode on a white horse. On the four cardinal points of the carousel, a knight sat in the outside saddle. These Four Horsemen, according to the sign at the entrance, would come to life to usher in the new world but, for now, rode steady vigil for all who follow the Lord and await His coming again.

I had barely stopped the stroller before Thibodeaux leapt from his seat and ran to the carousel's entrance. Fortunately it was one of the few rides without a height minimum. It was also one of the least popular at that point because we were able to climb aboard without a wait. Thibodeaux seemed to consider the saddle next to the horseman with considerable suspicion before choosing horses about three rows back. I helped him onto the outside horse while Molly climbed onto the one next to it. I stood between, holding hands from both horses as the ride began. I watched as a smile crept across first the child's face and then the mother's.

The world was spinning slowly and with it my idealized version of the divine, the interactions of key people in central narratives that spanned thousands of years, from the Garden of Eden to the Apocalypse of Revelations, the heights of Heaven to the depths of Hell, with gift shops and snack bars sprinkled in. And maybe my world, in some form or fashion, had been destroyed. Maybe I'd descended into Hell alongside Molly. And maybe we were rising again to new heights. Or maybe those were just abstractions and the human condition manifests both extremes simultaneously. The best of times is the worst of times. And maybe the best we can hope for is the enchanted smile of a kid engaged in the wonder of our universe. And we don't get that unless we forgive our brothers. And ourselves.

Made in the USA
Charleston, SC
09 December 2012